BACHELOR SEAL

Sleeper SEALs
Book 5

SHARON HAMILTON

SHARON HAMILTON'S BOOK LIST

SEAL BROTHERHOOD SERIES
Accidental SEAL (Book 1)
Fallen SEAL Legacy (Book 2)
SEAL Under Covers (Book 3)
SEAL The Deal (Book 4)
Cruisin' For A SEAL (Book 5)
SEAL My Destiny (Book 6)
SEAL Of My Heart (Book 7)
Fredo's Dream (Book 8)
SEAL My Love (Book 9)
SEAL Brotherhood Box Set 1 (Accidental SEAL & Prequel)
SEAL Brotherhood Box Set 2 (Fallen SEAL & Prequel)
Ultimate SEAL Collection Vol. 1 (Books 1-4 / 2 Prequels)
Ultimate SEAL Collection Vol. 2 (Books 5-7)

BAD BOYS OF SEAL TEAM 3 SERIES
SEAL's Promise (Book 1)
SEAL My Home (Book 2)
SEAL's Code (Book 3)
Big Bad Boys Bundle (Books 1-3 of Bad Boys)

BAND OF BACHELORS SERIES
Lucas (Book 1)
Alex (Book 2)
Jake (Book 3)
Jake 2 (Book 4)
Big Band of Bachelors Bundle

TRUE BLUE SEALS SERIES
True Navy Blue (prequel to Zak)
Zak (Includes novella above)

NASHVILLE SEAL SERIES
Nashville SEAL (Book 1)
Nashville SEAL: Jameson (Books 1 & 2 combined)

SILVER SEALS
SEAL Love's Legacy

SLEEPER SEALS
Bachelor SEAL

STAND ALONE SEALS
SEAL's Goal: The Beautiful Game
Love Me Tender, Love You Hard

BONE FROG BROTHERHOOD SERIES
New Year's SEAL Dream (Book 1)
SEALed At The Altar (Book 2)

PARADISE SERIES
Paradise: In Search of Love

STANDALONE NOVELLAS
SEAL You In My Dreams (Magnolias and Moonshine)
SEAL Of Time (Trident Legacy)

FALL FROM GRACE SERIES (PARANORMAL)
Gideon: Heavenly Fall

GOLDEN VAMPIRES OF TUSCANY SERIES (PARANORMAL)
Honeymoon Bite (Book 1)
Mortal Bite (Book 2)
Christmas Bite (Book 3)
Midnight Bite (Book 4 Coming Summer 2019)

THE GUARDIANS (PARANORMAL)
Heavenly Lover (Book 1)
Underworld Lover (Book 2)
Underworld Queen (Book 3)

AUDIOBOOKS
Sharon Hamilton's books are available as audiobooks narrated by J.D. Hart.

ABOUT THE BOOK

Medically discharged from the Teams, notorious bachelor SEAL, Morgan Hansen, is approached to lead the biggest undercover operation of his career. For credibility, he is tasked with training and partnering with his ex, from a breakup that made news headlines and nearly ended is career.

Women's empowerment guru, Halley Hansen, has built an empire around her live televised events and seminars. But her world-wide message for women has put her in the cross-hairs of some radical terrorist cells operating within the United States. The last person she wants to turn to or trusts is Morgan, her ex.

They bury their pain to work together for a cause bigger than the both of them. And if they don't implode in the passion of their re-connection, they just might have a chance to save the women of the world.

AUTHOR'S NOTE

It has been my pleasure to be part of this Sleeper SEALs series with other talented authors I've either worked with before, or known and admired. I always love creative projects where we each get to put our personal spin on the general theme. Some of my previous characters appear in this book, and the character Commander Greg Lambert appears in all of them.

I've been writing about SEALs righting wrongs in the Homeland since 2011, with my first SEAL Brotherhood book, Accidental SEAL, so this topic was not new to me. Of course we do not know of any super secret covert task force created by the CIA to protect our Homeland from our enemies, but it doesn't take much of a stretch to go there.

And we know that the SEALs are tasked with protecting the innocent all over the globe. This is a work of fiction. And in our world, they protect us at home as well as on foreign soil.

They are heroes uniquely qualified not because they are the brightest or strongest. They are the ones who don't quit, no matter what the odds.

I'll probably continue this story in the future, as the

writing muse takes over my life again. I hope you enjoy something I've certainly had a wonderful time writing for you.

Sharon Hamilton
Santa Rosa, California
November 14, 2017

I support two main charities. Navy SEAL/UDT Museum operates in Ft. Pierce, Florida. Please learn about this wonderful museum, all run by active and former SEALs and their friends and families, and who rely on public support, not that of the U.S. Government. www.navysealmuseum.org

IF YOU GOT ANY CLOSER, YOU WOULD HAVE TO ENLIST

I also support Wounded Warriors, who tirelessly bring together the warrior as well as the family members who are just learning to deal with their soldier's condition and have nowhere to turn. It is a long path to becoming well, but I've seen first-hand what this organization does for its warriors and the families who love them. Please give what your heart tells you is right. If you cannot give, volunteer at one of the many service centers all over the United States. Get involved. Do something meaningful for someone who gave so much of themselves, to families who have paid the price for your freedom. You'll find a family there unlike any other on the planet. www.woundedwarriorproject.org

CHAPTER 1

FORMER SEAL MORGAN Hansen looked over the sea of faces waiting for his initiation speech at the Rusty Scupper. Some faces were new, some old-timers—veterans of the love wars that could level a Navy SEAL as swiftly as an IED. And just like in a firefight, the Brotherhood needed the Band of Bachelors who would gather occasionally to mark a new milestone.

One by one, they were admitted into this little conclave, held up by buddies who had tasted the smell of blood and smoke, heard the screams of battle and the sighs of a night of aimless sex. Though they were all well-oiled machines, made up of bone and sinew, they walked into the firefights with their eyes wide open, ready to die so some of them—and most the rest of the country—could live. And they all had their own remedies to deal with the craziness and the intense excitement of their lives. Sometimes, it was coming home to a good woman and a family who worshiped them. But not all were that lucky.

And so Morgan's little celebrations were borne, creating some way for him to forget the cost, as well as a gateway to uncertainty. The purpose was not to create a compelling or exciting future like their past, but just to make sure there was a future at all. That was the hard part.

Losing your heart was just one of the prices you had to pay when you were a SEAL. And now Morgan couldn't even have that. Oh yes, he had the plank. He had the autographed pictures and his old gear, stashed in a box under the floorboards of his bedroom. It was a master bedroom in a house that only housed the master—never a place for women—since the mistress had left some nearly ten years ago. That spot remained unoccupied, not because he couldn't find anybody else to fill it, but because he wanted to prove to the world and himself that he didn't need it. Then perhaps he would. But he was honest with himself.

He wasn't there yet.

The beer flowed like it always did, sometimes with chasers, sometimes adorned with epithets and cursing as the bitter pill went down and made them all men of the Bachelorhood. They were always brothers, even with the married and attached SEALs. But it took a real man to be part of the Bone Frog Bachelorhood, and it was a helluva lot harder than most people thought to be one. Morgan would stare in the mirror each morning and say back to himself, "Here I am. I'm still here."

He held his glass up as the silence broke through the group, the background music still playing loudly. They observed the way his tense smile appeared, the way the hollows of his eyes were just a little deeper, the way the lines on his face became more and more pronounced as the years went by. And still they all watched him. He knew some worshiped him and the perceived peace he'd made of his life. If they only knew, they wouldn't think such good thoughts about him.

"Tonight, Gents, we are here to welcome another traveler to our little group, a man who has at last found his way to the fellowship of the Band of Bachelors. We're here to show him a good time and to make sure he understands what an important first step he has taken to put all that shit behind him."

Several of the guys in front began to snicker, and someone swore and didn't wait for the toast, downing his beer before Morgan could finish.

But the rest of them raised their glasses, shouted "Amens!" to the Viking gods who haunted all their places of drink worship, and inhaled, readying themselves for the communion of the dead, the walking dead, and the horned heroes of Oden who showed them how to overcome anything.

"To fuckin' Curtis Cronquist and his entry into the Bachelorhood."

"To fuckin' Curtis," they all said, with their own personal brand of exuberance. Whatever it was, it worked for all of them.

He'd found Curtis sniveling in the parking lot earlier and listened to him ramble about how he couldn't come to the celebration. It was too soon, Curtis had said. His eyes remained painfully bloodshot and his nose continued to run. His left cheek was still bright red from the slap across his face Morgan gave him in response. But Curtis stood up and received the catcalls, cheers, and toasts.

Morgan watched his shaking frame—Curtis' hand was on his beer glass in a grip so tight it might shatter while the other balled into a fist—and knew exactly how the man felt. He'd like to tell him the days and weeks would go by and with each passing week it would get better, but he'd made a promise to himself a long time ago he could lie or bullshit, but never to a Brother.

"Thanks, fellas."

His voice wavered a bit. Morgan wasn't going to let him continue and start saying things like, "This means a lot to me," another one of those unmanly things assholes told the world when they really felt like killing something or someone inside. So Morgan interrupted him.

"We're ten times stronger with you amongst us. Curtis here is a linguistics expert, and he's going to teach us how to say some nasty things in nearly twenty-two languages. Right, Curtis?"

"Fuckin'-A," Curtis said, but was drowned out by the cheering crowd. He added something Morgan did not know. "Danny Begay taught me how to say 'pig afterbirth' in Navajo. With the right voice inflection and hand gestures, that scares the shit out of the evil ones."

They knew there was a big difference between the few Afghans and Iraqis they could trust, along with their families and the majority of tribes who harbored generations of hatred for the "invaders." It was hardwired in their DNA and not their fault, Morgan thought. But that didn't mean he could forgive. He'd never forgive them for any of it.

When Curtis sat down and received the little tokens—some coins from whorehouses, mostly fake, challenge coins, patches, and vials of sand from hell—Morgan witnessed the normalcy of being single, yet again. It strengthened his own resolve, as if going through the threshold with poor Curtis was good energy for himself as well.

Well, fuck it, it was.

Outside, as they were leaving some two hours later, the brush of moist air fresh from the ocean kissed Morgan's face and almost made him think he was in the presence of some beautiful thing with soft creamy skin, puffy red lips, and a cleavage he could lose himself in with the promise of a safe ride to oblivion and no guarantees. It was his mind playing tricks on him again. Somewhere, a sea bird called. A couple of girls laughed, and he heard a male voice responding. These were not foreign sounds, but not anything that interested him.

Curtis was having trouble walking so Morgan threw his arm around the young SEAL's waist and hoisted him closer to keep him from hitting a streetlight or stop sign pole. "Come on, Curtis. Get your legs working just a little, and I'll do the balancing. But fuckin' give me some help."

Curtis struggled, trying to shake the help.

"Don't fuckin' try it, or I'll slap you again."

Curtis gurgled a chuckle, something halfway between a belch and a heave nearly swallowing his tongue, and then began to cough.

"And if you fuckin' puke on me, I'll remove all your clothes and make you walk home *nekked*. Your career as a SEAL will be over."

Unlike Morgan, Curtis was still attached to SEAL Team 3. Morgan loved those guys and seriously missed them, even after the years. He knew, although he spent most his time with the misfits and marriage failures of the Team, that connection still kept him whole. If a guy was on a downward spiral, he would soon lose his Trident, as well as his marriage, and that's what Morgan had created the Brotherhood for. To pick up the pieces. One could even say he was the garbage man of SEAL Team 3.

He heard a whistle from behind and saw Cody, the Scupper bartender tonight, signal and point to the street behind them. He'd called a cab. Fuckin' good thing, too, because Morgan couldn't remember where he'd parked his truck. He was only a little bit less drunk than Curtis. But it wouldn't be a career ender to get a DUI, like it would be for Curtis.

Having a taxi waiting was the best choice, and if he hadn't been so drunk, he'd have thought about it. Cody came running, taking on over half the load, and assisted getting them both inside. He handed the cabbie some money. Morgan was going to thank him, but his head jerked back when the cab sped up to supersonic speed. He turned around and out of the rear window saw Cody standing with his white apron and giving him the one-finger salute.

Well, he deserved that.

The Indian driver was oblivious to bag of bones he'd picked up. His little elephant idol and beads swung back and forth on the rear view mirror. His irises were dark in contrast to the white of his eyes that were almost too bright to view.

"Where to?" He was chewing on a toothpick.

"Uh, thirty-four forty-eight Apricot. Over in the Orchards Subdivision."

The cabbie took out his toothpick and stared back, having now observed the condition of his passengers based on the slurring of Morgan's speech. "I know it. I'll wake you when I'm there." And then he went back to his work, plowing through obstacles on this Saturday night, helping his precious cargo home safely. There were good cabbies and asshole cabbies in Coronado, and not many in-between. This one was a good one.

Morgan was yanked to attention when the cab stopped abruptly and he nearly hit the seat in front of him. The driver was over on Curtis's side first, which left Morgan to his own devices. But as soon as he saw the little bungalow he'd wisely invested in some dozen years ago, now surrounded by much larger, remodeled homes, he whipped his ego into shape and tried to look like he was coming home sober. He'd had a lot of practice at that during the years before his marriage failed. And he'd always been unable to fool anyone. It guaranteed him a cold couch and an angry woman at home, which was probably all he deserved.

But tonight it was all about helping Curtis, being the ferryman over the River Styx. His charge was giving the cabbie some attitude, which wasn't fair. Morgan came to his defense.

"Curtis, stop behaving like an ass. The man's trying to help you out. You're drunk, and I'm getting you to a bed you can crash on. So shut the fuck up and do what he says."

Curtis wrenched his head up like a newborn and tried to look around. "Where am I? I don't live the fuck here."

"Just close your trap and cooperate, you dumbass frog."

"But where am I?"

"What the fuck do you care? Just cooperate. Quite being so dumbass stubborn."

"Where are you taking me?"

"Curtis, I'm about to dump you right here on the sidewalk." They leveraged him forward, up the cute little brick walkway now bordered with weeds—the touch about the house that Morgan's former wife loved and probably the reason he bought it—and on towards the arched wooden door with the metal grates over the tiny windows he used to fantasize came from a Spanish prison. "This is my house. I'll take you home tomorrow."

Curtis stiffened again, stopping his forward progress. The cabbie swore under his breath.

"Whoa! I'm not that kind of guy. You got the wrong guy. And I'd never do a threesome, either!"

"Honest to god, Curtis, I'm about to revoke your membership to the Bachelor club. Just because we hate ex-wives doesn't mean we hate women or love men more. So burn that idea right out of your brain, you dumb fuck."

Curtis started to laugh. "Didn't think so. But you never know—"

"Just shut up and let us get you inside."

They hauled his frame down the wooden hallway to the master in the back, and his dragging feet brought all the area rugs with him like a child's blanket. After dumping him at the edge of the bed, Morgan was able to roll him back toward the center.

The cabbie was halfway through the living room when Morgan shouted something about payment, and then he remembered Cody paid the guy to begin with, probably with a generous tip too. Two drunkass SEALs could be a real pain.

The driver slammed the door, and the house was peaceful and completely silent, except for the revving of the driver's motor and the screech of his tires getting him out of Dodge.

The phone rang. Searching in the dark for the kitchen receiver, Morgan found it empty. He pulled his cell from his back pocket, saw a number he didn't recognize, and answered it.

"Who the fuck I don't know can call me at this hour?"

At first, the sound tickled his ear, but then Morgan began to make out the words. Only every other one.

"…wanted to stop by…..very dangerous and a little delicate….no hard feelings…Morgan, I'm sure you…." Then the words rattled off like the chattering of a chipmunk.

Morgan barely had enough energy to respond and wasn't sure the caller was speaking English. "Look, I can't hear you, and I'm in no condition right now. Call back in the morning—" Morgan dropped the phone and passed out on the floor.

CHAPTER 2

HALLEY HANSEN ARRIVED at the auditorium in a midnight blue limo an hour before her speaking engagement. She studied notes on her laptop, making a couple of last minute changes before sending the file to the program crew at the center to be uploaded to the teleprompters. Her cell phone chirped, and she smiled at the text message. She wanted to respond, but knew better than to detour at this critical moment.

The crowd was expected to be over ten thousand, and eighty-five percent of them would be women. She wanted her message on point, and she wanted to deliver it without shaking, as she was now.

Crystal Cortez, her new personal assistant, sat across from her, talking on the phone quietly. Halley waved to raise her attention as the driver swerved and was directed toward the rear of the convention center.

"Make sure they get my upload, Crystal. I just sent it."

"Of course." Crystal removed her hand from the phone and signed off her call quickly. She redialed another number and gave Halley a thumbs-up about a minute later. "Everything came through okay."

"Thanks." Halley scanned the sooty buildings adorned with spray paint artwork and gang tags she'd seen all over the US from her travels. The back alley-ways of these big venues were always the scariest places for her. They revealed the naked truth about the community and the area, without the adornments of the front of the centers, where lights and landscaping, tall columns of steel and granite, or pre-formed con-crete sculpted the building's Sunday morning best. Even this part of Orange County had its seedier spots, despite the billions of dollars being made every second here.

As they made their way up the rear ramp, they shared the space with two large delivery vans with a half dozen men unloading boxes of her books, her pink camo tee shirts, and other SWAG from the Halley's Heroes campaign. A local florist had delivered two large sprays of red roses, which were also being carried inside. As a motivational speaker, Halley used these "free" planned events to recruit more women looking to change and empower their lives. The money gener-ated from the tee shirts, CDs, books, and other items would pay for the venue. That gave her the chance to sell seminars and her Hero Summit weekend experience coming up next summer in Hawaii. It was, after all, a business, and Halley's business sold women on themselves.

"Makeup's ready for you, Halley. You've got an interview with a local Santa Monica station when you're done. That okay with you?"

Halley gave Crystal a wide smile. She liked how all this was turning out. "Great job. Way to kill two birds with one stone. I appreciate how you take initiative."

Crystal looked down at her lap as she hugged the clipboard to her chest.

"You be sure to give me the sales figures at the break, okay?"

"Will do. And if I can get another interview, are you available for something quick or do you need to meditate?"

"All I need is five minutes today. I can give them five minutes, as long as I get my five minutes afterward, just before I go back on."

"I'll see what I can set up. You'll tell me if you're going to need a suit change, right?"

"Let's plan on that being a yes," Halley answered her back.

Crystal's handsome twin brother, Orestes Cortez, who wore a tux that form-fitted his supercharged frame, opened the limo's rear door. Halley had resisted showing him she thought him extremely attractive, especially since she still told herself a man with biceps and shoulders like a Titan god could not be trusted. She'd had all that, and it got her nowhere.

But Halley gave Orestes her hand as she gracefully extricated herself from the limo, Crystal right behind.

"Miss Hansen," he said, as he crooked his arm and escorted her to the rear doorway, paying no attention to her and focusing all his attention to whomever they were near. It was his job not to watch, but to protect, and Halley was grateful Orestes took his job seriously. Her thigh brushed his, and then his adjustment revealed the hard edge of a sidearm strapped beneath his armpit.

At last they were on thick carpeting, lit by large crystal chandeliers. The light orchestral music playing in the background was just like every convention center or auditorium, but what was different was the faint scent of some kind of spice air freshener wafting through the ventilation system. If she closed her eyes, she'd almost feel like she was in the middle of a Kasbah or a Bedouin tent in the middle of a desert somewhere, lit by torches and the bright stars of the night sky.

The nervousness she felt became the overwhelming sense of adventure she was so addicted to. She'd mastered the art of speaking to large groups, making them each feel like she spoke just to each one of them.

The larger her audiences—and they were getting larger and larger—the more excited she got. She liked it when the stakes were very high.

Orestes opened a door for her, but did not release her elbow. Her shoulder barely grazed his iron chest, and the smell of a fresh shave and expensive cologne sent a little chill down her spine. She dared to look at him over her shoulder.

"Thank you, Orestes." His smile was crooked, barely visible under his trimmed moustache. "You took your time tonight, and I appreciate it. Thank you for honoring me that way."

"My pleasure, ma'am," he answered politely, glancing down to the carpet and avoiding eye contact. Crystal appeared between the two of them, and she took Halley's computer, placing it on the couch facing a large mirror ringed with lights illuminating the makeup chair. She then hung a garment bag inside a small bathroom at the end of the dressing room.

The makeup artist motioned to the chair, and Halley stepped up and seated herself as she heard Orestes leave.

"I'm Pat. I don't think we've met before, right?" the artist asked her.

"Don't believe so. I've not been here to this complex." Halley gave her some instructions on what she wanted done with her shoulder length blonde hair and how red her lipstick was to be. "Show her the suit, Crystal."

Her assistant unzipped the bag and revealed the royal blue suit Halley would be wearing tonight. Dark blue was her power color, and on a woman, it was more powerful than the black. She could always tell how familiar with her lessons the crowd was. If there was lots of blue, she had plenty of fans and converts in the audience. A bright audience adorned with unprofessional floral prints, even in Hawaii, meant Halley had her work cut out for her.

After finishing her makeup and donning her suit, the reporter from Santa Monica and one cameraman entered the dressing room. Halley offered them the couch, which the reporter took. Halley sat slightly elevated in the makeup chair as the cameraman moved all about the room, trying to avoid the glare from the lights.

"I'm with KRON4, Santa Monica, Greg Carver."

Halley could tell he was young and probably on one of his first assignments.

"Nice to meet you, Greg. You're very brave."

"Yes, well, I do what they give me to do." He had a youthful smile, which didn't cover up his nervousness. His blushed cheeks didn't help, either.

"Make it count," Halley said without batting an eye. "Make it the best of your career."

The reporter cleared his throat. "So pretend I know nothing about what you do. How would you explain to a man why women should take your seminars, why they shouldn't be threatened with what they'd learn?"

Halley chuckled. "Very good question, Greg. You're going to be good at this."

The reporter blushed again.

"It takes a strong man to have a relationship with a strong woman. Men who are not self-actualized think they don't want the competition. They want a relationship with someone who is easy to get along with, or so they say in public sometimes."

"But you think that's a lie, I take it."

"Exactly. They want *intensity*, not only in the bedroom, but the boardroom as well. They want to share their life with someone who has the capacity to totally change them, maybe occasionally knock them on their butts. They place themselves at the mercy of this strong woman when they are complete men. If they are juvenile, a woman's strength worries them. Makes them uncomfortable."

"So is this seminar about men or women?"

"It's about teaching women that they don't have to take a back seat. That they can be as strong and perhaps stubborn as they want to be. As they feel like being. And the right man will not find fault. In fact, he'll crave everything about her."

"That's an interesting premise. You think men tell themselves they want one thing, but really want another—I mean, all men?"

"They want a woman who makes them feel more of a man when they are around her. I teach women how to become self-sufficient and irresistible, to learn to dance with the big boys, and to walk across the room in their lingerie without blushing, because they like to see the impact it has on their man."

The reporter looked up at the cameraman. Halley could tell part of this was going to be edited out.

"The worst thing a woman can do is do all the right things—be the perfect partner, wife. She'll become boring to him. And that's okay if she doesn't want him. But if she tells herself he's important, it's the worst mistake they could make. It isn't about pleasing them; it's about making them *have* to chase you."

The cameraman lowered his camera, signaling the interview was done. Halley could tell the young reporter wanted to go on.

"Stay and listen to my talk. If you have questions afterwards, you can text my PA, and I'll try to answer, okay?"

Crystal handed the reporter her card. "Don't forget to mention we met here, and I'll get answers to whatever questions you'll have. Thanks for doing this."

As the pair left, a young woman with headphones entered. "Miss Hansen, you've got fifteen minutes. I'll knock when I need you."

Halley saw Orestes face behind her in the crack of the doorway. "Great. Will you double check and make sure the teleprompter is correctly working, and please give me the first sentence of my speech so I know you've seen it?"

"Sure thing. Be right back."

Halley removed her jacket, kicked off her heels, and lay back on the couch.

"Does she want me to go for a few minutes?" the makeup artist asked.

"You can stay. Just meditating for a bit," Halley answered before Crystal could.

Halley began her process. She saw herself mounting the steps to the stage. Rose petals were everywhere, and the bright lights were hot, but somehow reassuring. In her vision, she couldn't see the faces of the audience yet, but she would ask to have the house lights turned on during the question and answer portion of the first half. The teleprompters on both sides of the room were clear and easy to read. She stepped on the rose petals and felt the familiar squish as her shoe smashed the moisture out of them, releasing a fine aroma that now enveloped her. She opened her mouth and began her talk, like she always began her talks.

"Ladies. Start your engines."

CHAPTER 3

MORGAN STARTED WHEN the noise he thought he was hearing in the desert suddenly began rumbling beneath him, making his knees knock and upsetting his stomach. That's when he realized he'd been sleeping on the floor and the banging was coming from the front door, shaking the whole house.

He stood and nearly keeled over. The alcohol was still fresh in his system, despite the sleep he'd had. He brushed down his shirt, noticed he'd not removed his shoes all night, and unlatched the door.

The bright Coronado sun hit him square in the forehead, sending a laser beam that traveled through his skull, and felt like it curled his hair at the back of his head. Someone huge was standing in front of him.

"Morgan, you look like shit."

He recognized the voice, but, since his left eye was lazier than his right, couldn't focus on the gent's face. His instincts didn't kick into gear to ward off the guy, so he tried to relax and just let his body adjust. After rubbing his eyes, he chanced a squint, discovering it was his old SEAL Team 3 buddy Jay Johnson.

"J.J., isn't this a little early to be making a social call?"

"I see you're dressed already."

Morgan looked down at his clothes. "Yup. Never got undressed. We did another initiation last night."

J.J. didn't ask permission, stepping past Morgan into the living room and closing the door behind him. He craned his neck to examine the hallway. "You alone?"

Morgan had to think about that one. "Yes."

"Good. I'm making coffee first. You got any?"

Morgan rummaged through cupboards and then remembered he kept his coffee in the refrigerator. He grabbed the glass pot and began filling it with water. J.J. took it away from him, pouring it into the coffee machine. Morgan brought out his half and half and ground coffee, measured the dark brown, life-saving elixir, and turned the pot on.

Jay examined him like a piece of dirty laundry. "You better sit down for this."

Morgan obliged, taking a seat across the small breakfast table and staring at his former Teammate while the coffee bubbled and filled the room with life. He moved to retrieve some mugs, but J.J. commanded he stay seated. When his buddy brought over the steaming mugs and placed the half and half between them on the table, Morgan used his index finger to stir the light caramel-colored coffee and didn't feel a thing. Whatever he was going to be told, it was important and probably not anything he wanted to hear.

Before they could speak, the door to the bedroom opened, and Curtis Cronquist stumbled forward, buttoning his shirt. J.J. looked between the two of them.

"That's special. In the old days, it would have been—" J.J. began.

"I was barely conscious. Forgot. Don't read anything into it." Morgan's mood began to sour. "Jay Johnson, this is new bachelor Curtis Cronquist. Curtis, meet Jay, or do you guys know each other?"

"Nice to meet you, Jay."

"Likewise. You still active?"

"Yessir. Team 3 all the way," Curtis said as he shook hands with the seated former SEAL. "I'll just grab some coffee and then catch an Uber back over to the Scupper. That okay with you?" Curtis' hair looked like a well-used piece of blond Brillo pad.

"Sure," shrugged Morgan.

Curtis brought the pot over to the table, seeking requests for a fill-up. Morgan took another and added his usual pour of cream. The three of them stared at each other in the awkward silence after Curtis seated himself perpendicular to the two former Teammates.

"How long before you go over again?" J.J. asked.

"Four months. We start working up right away, even though we just got back." He hesitated at first then added, "Things are heating up."

"That's for sure. You take down the hive, and the bees fly all over the place looking to start a new colony," Morgan answered. "You said Africa this time, right?"

Curtis put his finger to his lips and then shrugged. "We're not really sure. I'll know more, depending on whether we work up in Reno, Alaska, or Mexico."

The two former SEALs nodded. Everyone was prepared to go when the call came, and it was a luxury if they knew more than a month ahead of time which part of the world they'd be going.

Morgan was curious what brought Jay over to the house. "Been like four or five years at least, J.J. How's life? Bet your kids are huge now."

J.J. smiled. He made a rounded motion to his belly. "Carmen is huge, too. This will be number four."

"Nice. You don't have to worry about being home for the birth. I missed both of mine," offered Curtis.

J.J. threw a serious glance at Morgan.

"I didn't have that problem," Morgan quipped back and then grinned. After another awkward silence, he asked his friend again. "So what brings you over here so early on a Saturday morning?"

"Oh, I was just in the neighborhood. Wanted to check up on my old friend."

"You the asshole who called me last night?"

J.J. rolled his right shoulder. "None other." His eyes were steady, and Morgan instantly understood J.J. needed to have a private conversation with him.

"Hey, fellas. I'm gonna head off," Curtis said as he stood, bringing them all to their feet. "Nice to meet you, man."

"You keep getting the bad guys for us, son."

Morgan knew it was a sincere wish.

"Every one I can nail. Due to my present circumstance, I like it better over there than here, except for the kids, of course. But I don't mind. Made for this shit."

"Shit yea," answered Morgan. "You take care." The two of them slapped backs, and Curtis was gone. Morgan turned around and saw J.J. take a deep breath. "Okay, what the fuck's up?"

"Sit down," came the answer. There was no eye contact.

"This something I need a little nip over?" Morgan could see, whatever it was, J.J. was having difficulty getting it out on the table.

"You don't need that. Maybe later after we talk."

Morgan sat, leaning back into the wooden chair. He just wanted to get it over with and suspected J.J. did as well.

"I was called back to Washington, D.C. You remember Navy Commander Greg Lambert?"

"Yessir. Hard to forget him or that fuckin' little bitch dog that bit my ass one night at a poker game. But I thought he retired."

"He did. Well, he's working in D.C. right now on a couple special projects with the Headshed, including those bugs at the CIA. A bunch of those guys are doing stuff that wasn't around when we were in. I haven't spoken to him since before we got out." J.J. looked down at his hands, folded on the wooden table. He brushed aside the coffee mug, leaned forward, and searched Morgan's face. "I'm not going to sugar coat it. You're not going to like it. Any of it."

"What's wrong? Someone bought the farm?"

"Not exactly." He paused again and bit his lip. Morgan could see he'd been tapping his left foot under the table. "They've got a unit created to do very covert, special projects. It's a counter-terror unit under the jurisdiction of the CIA, created to handle solo dark ops missions. Commander Lambert is heading up this new division."

"Projects? Projects for who?"

"These are dark ops missions, and they're only using former Navy SEALs, about a dozen of us. Anyway, I got recruited to the task force. I just got my first mission."

"So you're back on the Teams?"

"Not exactly. Like I said, this is covert, strictly a need-to-know operation. I get caught, they don't know anything about it type of thing. And it's mostly based in the Homeland. It was the brainchild of mini-POTUS himself."

"The Vice President? You're talkin' the Homeland? Fully authorized?" Morgan had heard whispers, but he thought they were just ghosts of ideas that were always surrounding them all or wishful thinking, since he wasn't active any longer.

"Like I said, not exactly fully authorized. Covert."

"Why would you do something like that with your wife and all those kids? You're teaching, right?"

"High School Administration. I'm already Assistant Principal."

"Geez. So why tell *me*? And why did you take on something like that?"

"Because of who it involves. I'd be protecting one of our own. And, well, I miss the action. Don't you?"

Morgan ignored his question. "*Our* own? Who are we talking about, J.J? I'm wide awake now."

"This mission concerns your wife—er—your ex, Halley."

Morgan got to his feet and grabbed J.J. by the collar, pulling his torso over the table, spilling a coffee mug. "You leave your hands off Halley, you dumb fuck."

Jay extricated himself from Morgan's grip, straightened his shirt. "Sit down," he commanded. "There's more. And if you don't get a hold on yourself, I'm going to leave, and I'll come back later when you're not so volatile."

Morgan grabbed a towel, wiped up the coffee spill, and dumped his frame back into the chair.

"They asked me to do this job, and I said no. Not until I talked to you. We have a code, all of us. I'd expect the same if the situation was reversed."

Morgan's gut burned. He needed some food in his belly. A wave of nausea washed over him and then left him cold and clammy. "So when the fuck are you going to tell me?"

"Commander Lambert said they had intel that some bad actors are planning something on Halley."

"You mean like kidnapping?"

"Or worse. A big event. Something showy." J.J. leaned in again and whispered, "Another 9-11 event, Morgan."

He'd spent so much time burying all his feelings for Halley he'd been left numb. Trying to unpeel all the icepacks from his head and chest, and especially surrounding his heart, he found he just didn't have any reaction at all, except some ancient primordial territorial thing flopping around his belly. The dang thing was black, laughing like some wild-assed monkey biting its own tail. It was crazy, and it made no sense. He couldn't focus on what it was exactly he did feel. He gave himself a mental slap and then returned J.J.'s worried stare.

"When?"

"That's just it; we don't know. But it could be any day now."

"How long have you known about this?"

"I just flew home last night. I called you when I landed. Morgan, I couldn't do this mission without informing you. Lambert forbid me to contact you, but I told him I'd turn it down unless I talked to you first."

"Why Halley?"

"Because she's a high profile target, Morgan. Former model, actress, and wife of a Navy SEAL flying all over the world, giving these seminars, doing workshops, and speaking to women. You know there are people who don't like that sort of thing, Morgan. We met some of them overseas, and we saw firsthand what they did to their children and wives."

The pictures were still vivid in Morgan's mind, though it had been ten years.

"We can't do anything about the small cell attacks

like the one in Portland. At least, not today we can't. But the CIA doesn't want another big one."

Morgan's head spun.

"I won't take the job unless you give me your blessing," J.J. added.

"Well, I won't."

"I was afraid of that." J.J. leaned his forehead into the palm of his hand then let his fingers slip into and rub his curly scalp. He positioned his hand beneath his chin. "I know you better than to think you'd want any harm to come to her, even though you had a rough separation—"

"That's an understatement. More like an earthquake. We never should have married. We are two people who absolutely would have killed each other if we'd stayed together. Shoot, the more efficient thing would be to let them get us back together. I'm a one man wrecking crew, trust me."

"I get it."

"No. You don't. Because I have a problem."

"What's that, Morgan?"

"Even though she hates me—I mean, truly hates me—I can't allow anyone else to make her miserable or to end her life."

"Not surprised to hear that."

"So the only way I'd give permission is if I go instead."

"No can do, Morgan. That's explicit—all the way from the Vice President, perhaps even the President himself."

"Then we have to go together."

"That's not what I came here for."

"Doesn't matter. Those are my terms."

J.J. sighed. "I will ask. But I'm sure of the answer. If you can't let me take this job, I'm going to quit the task force. So I'll ask. No promises, okay?"

"No, you'll *tell* them. You'll tell them I insist."

"Well, there's one other problem. She has a fairly serious boyfriend."

Morgan thought about that, envisioning him strangling the boyfriend in front of her. He'd have to temper his anger and his thoughts if he had any chance of being effective.

"Can I ask you, Morgan, why you care? Other than for old time's sake? You must have calculated what it would be like to see her again, to perhaps be her friend?"

"I can't be her friend or boyfriend, J.J. And certainly not her husband. I'm done with that. That's all gone and turned to ashes years ago. But I'm not done being her protector. I was made for that. And I know her so well no one would have a chance to get to her if I'm around."

"It will be complicated with the boyfriend."

"No worries there. So she's married? Never would have figured that one." Morgan wished he'd not brought it up. He didn't really want to know. Or so he told himself.

"No, not married. Not even engaged."

It wasn't right that Morgan felt an inkling of something like manly ego. He'd been somewhere with Halley the boyfriend hadn't been.

He'd walked the plank.

He deserved all the hell this mission was going to cost him, if they let him do it. He'd bought and paid for it. His heart, that old withered thing, had never really recovered, either.

CHAPTER 4

H ALLEY HANSEN MET her driver at SFO, and on the hour-long trip to Los Altos Hills, she checked her phone for voice messages. She expected at least one. But it wasn't there when she landed, wasn't there when she gathered her bags at the carousel, either. Now, seated in the rear of the black limo, she still found no communication from Gibril.

One of her rules was to never leave a message for a man, making him feel confined, unless the message had been prearranged. She decided to dial his number, planning to hang up if she got his voicemail.

Their relationship had deepened in the past few months, but they were still learning each other's rules and boundaries. The little game of cat and mouse, revealing more and more personal details about each other as they explored their bodies, was delicate, slow-moving, and very passionate. But she did feel like she was holding her breath a lot.

After her fiasco of a marriage to Morgan, she'd not let anyone come close. Now that it was happening again, she was nervous, apprehensive, but very excited. Her handsome, billionaire investor boyfriend made the stars sparkle just a little bit brighter these days and put a bounce in her step.

Expecting to get his message line, she was shocked when Gibril Messi picked up on the second ring. His polished English accent from years at boarding school in London, with a touch of his Middle Eastern dialect, made her melt on the inside.

"Awww, how's my beautiful princess today? You must be back from Los Angeles?"

"Just on my way home now."

"I missed you. Found myself thinking about you all day."

"Really? And what were you thinking?"

"I was dreaming about going for a walk in the woods, perhaps with a bottle of wine and a basket full of gourmet goodies."

"Hmm. Sounds nice."

"In my daydream, I watched you pluck the grapes from my fingers."

Halley's spine tingled as she heard his deep baritone voice, letting it vibrate everything delicate inside her. She suddenly felt flushed and awakened. But she held her excitement at bay, which only heightened the experience.

"Gibril, how about we enact that little drama tomorrow afternoon? Tonight, I just want to unwind, take a bath, and go to bed early." It was important she not appear too eager for his company, but Gibril was slowly becoming an addiction she didn't mind having.

"Excellent idea. I have a fundraiser to attend this evening, so tomorrow will be perfect!"

A tiny bit of angst crept into her gut. He'd never mentioned this before, and she had not been previously invited.

Gibril quickly filled the silence. "How was it? Exhausting??" His buttery words made her hang on every syllable. He was good at changing the subject at just the right time.

"It went very well, thank you. I'm nearly filled up for the October event, and I have three weeks still to go."

"Brava, my dear. You are irresistible!"

"Well, I don't know about that, but I'm glad the Summit will be a success and most likely sold out, too." Halley's curiosity returned, and she bent one of her own rules. "Gibril, what's the fundraiser for?"

"Oh, it's a benevolent society my family has contributed to for years. Way too boring for you, I'm afraid. Mostly old men giving lots of speeches. I'll tell you all about it tomorrow."

Satisfied, she began the sign-off. "Call me back in the morning to confirm, okay?"

"Absolutely. Have a wonderful evening and a glass of wine for me, and maybe burn an extra candle?"

She found his exotic language and culture, stories of his family back in Sudan, and his gentle, attentive ways a pure pleasure to be around. His hands were smooth, nails trimmed, and manicured. He wore lemon oil cologne and had a tall, lean body, which was always impeccably dressed.

She wasn't going to overthink anything.

After the disaster of her first marriage, this budding romance was a welcome change in her life, and about time, too. Morgan had constantly pushed her into overload in so many ways with his hulking body, his big callused hands, a sexual appetite that matched hers, and his secrets and loyalty to his brothers. She had to run in her high heels just to keep up with him on a daily basis. Halley had known she would forever be sharing Morgan with the rest of his SEAL Team. Being married to him had been like training for a marathon that would never end.

The driver pulled into her gated entrance. Halley used her clicker to open the first gate just off the road, which she shared with one other neighbor. At a fork, where the shared road ended, the driver turned right, stopping for her to open the second gate with a scan of her iPhone. After the short drive to the entrance, he parked and quickly moved to the rear to open the door for her. She stepped out into the warm afternoon glow, surveying her view from the walkway to her front door. On display was the entire San Francisco Bay: from San Jose to San Francisco. The sky was blue, dotted with tufts of billowy clouds. A promise of rain was in the air, but otherwise, the view was unblemished by haze.

Once inside her tiled foyer, she thanked her driver and handed him a hundred dollar bill, which was her custom. He tipped his hat and was on his way. Setting the bags inside her small elevator, she sent them to the landing upstairs outside the master bedroom, just before she went into the kitchen to get a glass of wine and a light supper.

She checked the Los Angeles station and watched the clipped interview she had with the reporter yesterday afternoon. Her cell phone signaled a text from Crystal Cortez.

'You made it home okay?'

'Yes, sorry I didn't text sooner. Just getting ready to fix something and then take that nice bath I've been dreaming about. You two made it to Las Vegas?' Halley texted her in return.

'Yes, my mother was so surprised to see us both. We got tickets to see "O" tonight.'

'Well, have a well-deserved weekend off. Give Mama Cortez a hug from me. Thank you for everything. Give Orestes a hug as well. We did great. Send me the numbers on Monday

when you get them.'

'Will do. I'm thinking you're sold out.'

'Love that thought. Talk Monday.' Halley ended it with a heart, and it was returned with the same.

She pulled out her laptop and made a note to ask Crystal to get a link to the interview to use in their promotions, and then shut her screen down. She put together a small tossed salad, heated up some leftover lasagna, and poured a glass of red wine while the news program continued.

There had been another terrorist attack in Oregon where a small school bus had been stolen and had plowed into a host of afternoon tourists down by the waterfront. Seven dead, many more wounded. Her heart ached for the innocent loss of life, including the life of an early responder who had been shot before the terrorist was felled. The details sent a cold shiver of fear down her spine as she surveyed the horizon, noticing the buildings in the East Bay reflecting an amber glow as the sun dropped.

She lived here all alone and loved this house. The perch with the fantastic view of the Bay was good for her serenity. Above all the bump and grind of the cities below, all the freeway traffic in the Hills, she felt comforted by the space, as if the crime and drama of the world was far away from her. Halley considered what might happen if her relationship with Gibril deepened further. Would she someday share this space with a man?

For the right man, yes!

There had been those of her friends who didn't understand her friendship with Gibril, and though they never said anything to her, she knew they had opinions. She'd seen the looks the two of them got when they strolled down the Boardwalk in Santa Cruz and browsed for antiques in Saratoga. But Northern California was filled with Middle Eastern citizens, as well as people from all over the world; Silicon Valley was a magnet for the bright, the successful from everywhere. But still, there were those looks. She felt them on her back as they passed by others.

Gibril had often mentioned how unfortunate the radicals had found such a lucrative method of drawing attention to their causes. He'd told he it had interfered with his work on occasion. There were some clients the company didn't have him work with because of his background. The two of them had discussed how this was so unfair. Halley was convinced he was the brightest partner in the treasure trove of startup geniuses at Focus Forum, the largest venture capital firm in the Valley.

Wow them with your unlimited ability to be brilliant, and they will receive you like a conquering queen. She spoke those words many times on stage to underprivileged women all over the world. *You are not bound by the limits of others' perceptions of you as a woman, as a leader, as a business person. Let those thoughts be their limiting beliefs, not yours.*

Well, these words applied to men as well.

Gibril understood this to be true, and it was part of the reason she loved being with him. His family had weathered many storms, coming from a rich culture and dynasty, having lost their fortunes and their lands many times, yet always bouncing back over the centuries to reclaim what was rightfully theirs. He could trace his roots back nearly five hundred years. In Gibril's family were the seeds of rugged determination and perseverance, like what she tried to bring to women in her Success Summits. Perhaps someday, it would be appropriate for Gibril to tell his story to her followers.

But not yet. The world was too polarized by divisions and hatred and, just like Gibril had mentioned, small-minded evil-doers who only wanted to wreak havoc with those more fortunate, enslaving those who would try to break out of the pattern of bigotry and clannish hatred. She'd spoken to women who wanted to attend her money-making sessions, only to let her know that they were not allowed to do so by the patriarchs of their family.

She turned off the television, rinsed her dishes, poured another full glass of Cabernet, and headed for her bedroom suite upstairs. Passing the elevator grates, she decided to unpack her suitcases in the morning. Tonight, she wanted to meditate in a warm bath by candlelight and dream about all the things that could be in her fantasy world.

She chose the rose bath salts and the bright pink rose-scented candle Gibril had brought her on their trip to Monterey. Slipping beneath the warm bubbles, she put a cool washcloth over her eyes and leaned back to meditate on that perfect world.

It didn't take long before her walk in the woods came to view. At first, she was alone. Then Gibril was at her side, which had recently been happening. She just allowed the vision to proceed without trying to direct it. As they stepped on hand-hewn wooden planks through the virgin rain forest, a light mist fell around them and fed the tall redwoods. Bird calls echoed throughout, as well as sounds of small animals burrowing beneath the planks and scurrying up the bark of the majestic trees. Occasionally, a winged insect would fly by on its mission to somewhere deep in the forest. She was always moved to tears when she saw this place, her perfect place.

As they walked through the foliage, the trees became tall ferns and the sounds of the ocean took over the forest symphony. She could feel the ebb and flow pulling at her heart, her stomach, willing her legs to walk along the wooden path until her bare toes hit warm sand.

She faced a sunset on the white waters of the surf, the breeze in her face, but she could still smell the thick green forest at her back, supporting and protecting her from harm.

Then his arms were about her body, strong and protective. She leaned into his chest and felt the brisk inhale and a vibration like a hushed moan given involuntarily. The warmth of his body set her insides aglow as she surrendered to the cloud of protection he gave her. He placed his face against her cheek, the early stubble of a beard startling. His lips kissed her neck. His strong fingers plied the muscles at the top of her spine and shoulders, massaging and smoothing out all the kinks, all her rough patches and all the places where she had imaginary sharp angles and pains. Everything was releasing as she let her self go, totally becoming one with his motions, with his kisses.

One hand slipped beneath her shirt, smoothing up her back, fingers kneading each vertebra. She turned so that his hand would cover her breast. With her eyes still closed, she felt him pull her towards him, heard his mouth open as he pulled her to his lips.

It suddenly occurred to her that she was tasting forbidden fruit, but the sweetness of his tongue and the need in her soul would not let her stop. Everything was safe. Everything was resolved. Every passion fulfilled or promised. Every certainty discovered and underscored. She was home as she took from him and then fed him back.

Until, in her daydream, she opened her eyes. The man standing before her was Morgan Hansen, her ex. And though she'd worked for over ten years to eliminate him from her memory and her life, today, he was right there as deeply embedded in that familiar way she now remembered. And she knew he would be impossible to replace, or ever forget.

CHAPTER 5

"**Y**OU'RE NOT GOING to convince him, Morgan. This is a fool's mission." J.J.'s forehead sweated as his large paw gripped the handle on the passenger door. Morgan knew he was driving fast, and it tickled him to think he could still scare one of his best friends of all time.

J.J. had made the call, and all holy hell had broken loose at the CIA. Commander Lambert was flying out to set things straight, and he'd warned J.J. that he'd just violated one of the most important tenants of his new job—secrecy. No matter what, Morgan thought J.J. had balls the size of an elephant's to stand up to Commander Lambert.

"Cool it, J.J. Wouldn't be manly to piss your pants."

"Fuck you. You don't scare me. It's just that this guy flying out here to tell you no is a big deal. And it might affect everything. Have you been listening to the news? That attack in Portland only makes what this special Team is doing all the more important, and something that needs to be kept secret. They're not going to jeopardize things for your whim."

"It's not a whim, and you know I have a good reason, J.J."

"Fuck! You're so pig-headed."

"You knew this when you knocked on my door yesterday morning. When you revealed to me what you'd been asked to do. Don't claim you didn't."

"Did you ever consider they'd deny adding you onto the team and can me at the same time? Then where would you be? You'd be having to sit on your hands—*ordered* to sit on your hands while some other asshole was out there trying to protect your ex—someone you didn't even know or trust."

"Then I'll get to him. Somehow I'd find out who they assigned, and I'd get to him. I'm not going to back down, J.J."

"The Commander says they wouldn't hire anyone but a former SEAL. And he can't hire an active duty frog. That's strictly prohibited. How the hell are you going to find him then? Or try to do this on your own? You can't, Morgan. You'll go to prison."

"Hasn't stopped some," Morgan mumbled.

"But not for an official high-level mission. And most the time, we keep it quiet because it was an oversight. Come on, Morgan. You know how it works."

"We all know there are the Team rules, the Head-shed rules, the official version, and then public opinion."

"And now there's your rules, Morgan. They're not going to go along with it."

"Doesn't matter what they do. I'm not giving up on the idea of leading a team to uncover the plot that may or may not be real."

J.J. screwed up his nose. "Oh, I think it's real alright. Again to my point about the Portland attack. Things are escalating. You know they are. And now you know something you shouldn't have. He'll probably let me have it both barrels. They'll tie my ankles to an anchor, and I'll be buried somewhere in Coronado Bay."

"Since when do you get intimidated by desk jockeys?"

"Lambert was a sonofabitch, Morgan. You knew him when he was in the field. He's no desk jockey."

"I wouldn't change my mind if the President of the United States called me."

"And you'd go to prison, Morgan. That could happen."

"If they found me."

"So what if he shows up with a detail of guards? Take you in? Morgan, you better get a Plan B formulated in a hurry if you don't want to get blindsided or react and do something you'd regret."

"Plan B is for losers."

"You don't mean that. On the Teams, we always had a Plan B, Plan C, all the way to the All-Hell-Fuckit-Plan-Z, remember? Nothing ever worked out the way we thought it would. And we trained for every eventuality. This makes no sense. You're not in shape, you've not lead a team in years, and I doubt anyone would want to go with you at this point. You're an old man, Morgan. Face the facts."

Morgan took a quick glance at his friend. "Tell me you don't mean that." He tried to make it sound softer, but the loudness of his Hemi Diesel truck motor drowned out their conversation. His anger was creeping in, and he knew he'd have to work at reeling it in a bit. "J.J., when was the last time you lead a team? And you're saying you wouldn't trust doing a mission with me? Really?"

J.J. scowled but didn't say anything intelligible.

"Where is this place?"

J.J. stared at the GPS on Morgan's dash. "Says we passed it back there. Oh wait. It's on the left, right there."

Morgan did an illegal U-turn, his fat truck tires on the right jumping the curb. He nearly took out a sapling that had been recently planted. Lawn was beginning to poke through brown mulch thinly laid down. The recent landscape job was simple, precise, and had all the earmarks of pure Federal Government.

He found the parking lot and drove to the gated entrance guarded by a two-man sentry of Federal Police, one handling incoming cars and one handling cars leaving the lot.

Morgan rolled down his window and squinted at the pinkish-skinned kid in the CIA Police uniform. "Ghostbusters" they were sometimes called by the Team guys.

"We're here to see Commander Greg Lambert."

The young guard checked his watch list screen. "I need proper identification, gentlemen."

Morgan and J.J. handed over their California Driver's licenses.

The guard had them both sign a guest pass, filled out with their license information, and replaced them with a pass card to place in the truck and two visitor badges.

"Put this on the Driver's Side, and park in one of the striped visitor slots over to the left. Your entrance to the building will be the double glass doors right in front of the parking lot. Have a good day, gentlemen."

Morgan placed the placard on the dash and turned to park where he'd been told. Before they climbed out of the truck, J.J. grabbed his arm.

"You aren't packing, right?"

"Of course not. You think I'm stupid? I keep everything under the floorboards."

"And no knives either, right?"

"J.J., I have been around the block a time or two."

"One more thing," J.J. added, ignoring Morgan's comment. "Stay calm. You get angry, you probably get hauled to jail. We're talking top secret stuff here. This is not a high-level facility, which means they don't trust us worth shit. We'll get to see that stuff if we're accepted into the fold."

"I thought this was totally covert. You changing your story, J.J.?"

"For all anyone else knows, you're applying to become a Federal Agent or join the CIA Police force. Wouldn't be the first former SEAL to try to go for that."

Morgan knew former SEALs were not likely candidates for the FBI or the CIA. They had too much rogue, and the Agencies felt they'd not had enough discipline and supervision to be proper recruits. Everyone he knew of who had applied had never gotten beyond the first interview.

"Thanks for the tip," he muttered to J.J.

Inside the glass doors, they were greeted by a huge metal detector and two more uniformed Police, both armed. They put their keys and wallets into a tray, which was scanned prior to the body scan they walked through. Morgan wasn't surprised when the buzzer went off, since he'd had a metal hip replacement just before detaching from the teams ten years ago. He was subjected to a limited body search, as the officer moved the wand over his hip and pelvis after Morgan lifted his shirt to show the large scar from the surgery.

Once cleared, he waited for J.J.'s turn, which also triggered a buzzer. J.J. had had an elbow and shoulder reconstruction with a plate in his forearm holding together his ulna, which had been broken in several places from an IED explosion in Afghanistan. It also left a sliver of metal embedded in his skull above his right ear that was not life threatening but could not be removed without causing brain damage.

They were both shown to Conference Room B, which was really an interview room not much larger than a big walk-in closet. They had a seat behind a gray table someone had sliced initials into. It had a gray government-issue label on the side, which someone had tried prying off.

The door sucked open, and Lambert stepped in, wearing civilian clothes but still looking all-military. His gray slacks and Navy blue zipper jacket, without a logo of any kind, were ironed crisply. His boots sported the high polish consistent with his rank.

Morgan considered getting to his feet, as J.J. did, out of respect of Lambert's position, but Lambert frowned and commanded his buddy sit.

"Okay, Hansen. What's this horseshit about you going on this ride with Johnson here? I told him it was a bad idea to even involve you in the first place, and you can see I was right."

"No, sir. I think J.J. was right to tell me."

"Well, I'm not quite sure how we'll reward that. Mr. Johnson here was preselected for this special group. You weren't considered—your name never came up. I'm here to give you the courtesy of telling you in person. The answer isn't just *no*; it's *hell* no. I want to be sure you don't say or do something to ruin the whole program. This isn't like being on a Team and you guys striking out to do some dumb shit like you used to do. This is something that could take down a whole administration if it isn't handled right. So, Hansen, I'm just going to be frank with you so we don't waste each other's time. You're not stable enough to be on this mission."

"And how's that, sir?"

"I've read your file." He tapped his finger on a gray folder labeled *S.O. Hansen, M., Retired*. "I know it's not complete and probably filled with holes, but it's a quickie profile I don't think you'll be too proud of. I understand fully why you weren't considered."

Morgan fisted and unfisted his right hand beneath the table clandestinely.

"You're pretty busy with your Bone Frog Brotherhood shit—the losers who beat up their wives and then go cry in their beer and relive the glory days. You assholes don't fool me one bit."

"Sir—" J.J. tried to insert himself.

"Shut up, Johnson. I'll get to you in a minute."

Morgan had had enough. He inhaled and tried to soften the blast of words he wasn't going to hold back any longer. Disrespecting his little gatherings, disrespected the men who had lost a part of themselves while they were serving. "I'm helping the guys who couldn't make it when they got home, sir. The ones who gave their all to the Navy—are still doing it, in some cases—but lost their families. With all due respect, sir, I don't know a one of them who has beaten up a woman, and if they ever did, they wouldn't be a part of the group. Now, if that makes me a loser, then I'm a proud loser."

Lambert blinked several times, sitting erect. "They got counselors for that crap, Hansen. Who made you the God of getting guys straight in the head after a divorce?"

"I make sure they get that, too. For some, I'm all they've got."

Lambert slumped back in his seat, crossed his arms, and studied the two of them. His eyes roamed mostly on Morgan.

"You think you're pretty smug with that answer, Hansen?"

"No, sir. I'm just one of the ones who help them heal. At least that's what I tell myself, anyway. There wasn't anything like that for me, so I created it. And who the fuck else wants to do it? Can you tell me that? Besides, they make good drinkin' buddies."

After a pause, Lambert leaned back to the table, tapping his right hand on the plastic top. He took a long time before answering. "Well, I think I owe you a bit of an apology, then, son. We didn't quite look at it that way in Washington, D.C. I'm sorry we didn't consider your sensitive feelings."

The Commander was picking a deliberate fight.

"I got nothing left to live for, sir. With all due respect."

J.J. even looked over at him, shock painted all over his face. Tension in the room was about to make the fluorescents pop.

"That's not exactly the requirement we need for acceptance into the division. We got ways of making decisions in Washington, and they go way beyond your fucking needs."

"Well, I wouldn't know about that. I'm not exactly schooled in politics, and I don't plan to be anytime soon, either."

Morgan could see the Commander was wavering,

though he didn't want to show it. He figured it was lethal to one's career to make a decision to add a member to the team without proper vetting from above. But he also guessed that the threat level was so high, the potential loss of life so potentially tragic, that having an inside track to the main focus of the terrorists might save them expensive mistakes. He was rewarded when Lambert responded. It was the opportunity he needed to make his final point.

"So, Hansen, tell me why I should let you work with Johnson here on this mission? Why should I trust you with something so delicate it could end not only my career, but several other men I serve with and care deeply about? Could bring down an entire administration."

Morgan matched the quiet way Lambert had come back to the table. He made sure his voice didn't contain a bit of anger, frustration, or fear. "Because if, as J.J. says, terrorists are after Halley, the last person in the world they'd expect to come to her aid would be me. That is, if they've done their homework. And I think if they're planning something big, someone is working on good intel and doing lots of homework."

"You've told him the details?" Lambert asked J.J., the anger now washed from his face.

"Not much of them, sir. I wasn't going to do that until I had your approval. But frankly, there weren't that many details to give him."

"I had a feeling this would happen," quipped Lambert. "You SEALs are as thick as thieves the way you stick together. Even after your service. You don't mix much with the active guys—"

"They don't let us, sir." J.J.'s hands flopped all over his lap. His friend was nervous as hell.

J.J. was right. It was painful talking to someone who was still on a team, dying to know about missions they were going on, what was happening out there in the sandpit and the battlefields of insanity, and seeing that look in their eyes. They knew you itched for the old days, thought Morgan. Especially those who didn't have an exciting life to lead afterwards. The active SEALs realized in a few years they'd be there, too.

Morgan could see Lambert understood that longing for action that would always be there, inside the heart of a true SEAL. The experience of working with men who would give their all to protect you was unlike any other job that ever could be. He hadn't appreciated that fully, until it was all over and he was out.

"I want to defend the woman who gave me a few years of her life. All of it, at least the first part, wasn't so unpleasant. I think partly it was my fault. I brought out the angry bitch side of her, not the side I thought I was getting. But that's all water under the bridge. She doesn't deserve this, Commander Lambert. No matter our differences, she's still an innocent, like all the other innocents in this world. If I didn't think I could be at my peak performance, if I wasn't up to it, I wouldn't even ask." Morgan was satisfied with himself. It came out better than he'd expected.

"Ask? Are you *asking*?" Lambert's eyebrows rose, but all other expression was absent.

"Yes. I'm asking. I'm telling you I'm asking."

J.J. started to snicker, and Morgan punched him hard in the arm, nearly sending him reeling off the chair.

Lambert's steely blue eyes fixated hard on Morgan again. The man was looking for cracks, holes, or lumps—anything he could sense that would override what he was about to do. Morgan knew he'd be pulling for giving him the chance. But Lambert didn't yet know this.

"I'm going to sleep on this. Lucky for you, there isn't anything indicating you've had a problem with the law, or I'd not even consider it. I head back to Washington tomorrow morning. I'll let you know my decision before then."

"Over pancakes. I like pancakes," Morgan blurted out.

"What the fuck—?"

J.J. was quick to jump in. "Everything goes better with lots of syrup and butter, Commander Lambert.

It's how we do things. You'll see. Anything you gotta say to us you can say tomorrow morning over pancakes. We go to the Scupper."

Lambert stood, and both Morgan and J.J. did the same. He extended his hand. "I always think a face to face meeting is best, even if it's bad news. So if you have the balls to get really bad news with your pancakes, I guess I can stomach the Scupper. I used to hang out there myself when I was going through school here in Coronado, but I never had pancakes there."

On the drive back to pick up J.J.'s truck at Morgan's house, the two discussed what they might need to get ready.

"You're pretty confident about his decision, aren't you, Morgan?"

"Come on, J.J. You know you are, too."

"Yes, I have to admit when we walked in there I didn't think it was going to work. But you kept your cool."

"Nah. That wasn't keeping my cool. That was telling the truth. My doing this is like giving hope to all those other guys who don't have something to do after the Teams. We all say we're glad we're done, but we aren't, are we?"

J.J. didn't answer, but Morgan could tell the hesitation to leave the cab of the truck signaled his agreement.

"Every man wants to feel useful, J.J. Even when we're disrespected. If we're useful, life is worth living. And it's the only way to reclaim what we experience as being gone. Because it can come back. I do believe it can come back."

"I sure hope you're right, Morgan. I definitely don't want to see Commander Lambert covered in pancakes and maple syrup, because that's what he'll get if he says no."

"So now do you see why we don't want a Plan B? That. That thing you just described. That scene would be painful."

CHAPTER 6

HALLEY AWOKE LATE. The night had been a long one, and the visions of Morgan's ghost standing behind her in her sacred space had stirred memories she'd needed to remain buried. She also took it as a warning. Was she feeling unsafe? Is that what that dream meant?

She stretched, preparing for a five mile run down her driveway, up the hill, and across one of the streets that bordered the hillside subdivision. It was a challenge on any morning, especially the steep hills, but today, she had the added burden of constantly glancing over her shoulder, as if someone were watching her every move. She rotated her shoulders and moved her neck from side to side, and still she couldn't shake off the uneasy feeling that followed her everywhere she went.

Normally, she'd be looking at gardens or admiring the view of the ever-changing Bay and the way the water glistened on it. Some days, it would be bright blue, others a greenish gray. Today, nothing piqued her interest.

When she twisted her ankle on a small rock her right foot came down on, she limped for several strides and then gave up, walking the rest of the distance to her home. Inside the front door, she locked the bottom lock, as well as the deadbolt. She *never* did that!

After a quick shower, she changed into a new workout set and propped her ankle on a chair with a bag of frozen peas covering it while she ate her breakfast, once again turning on the television.

The Sunday programs were still splashing sensational pictures and discussing the attack in Portland. She had several friends in the area, and she decided later on she'd give them a call. It was difficult to get her eyes unstuck from the horrible images plastered over and over again on the screen.

And then it hit her. She was falling for the fear, the weight of the world on her shoulders. Her lightness, her power, was untapped this morning. She needed to meditate and find that sweet spot of confidence and possibility.

Wow them with your unlimited ability to be brilliant and they will receive you like a conquering queen.

She flipped off the television and vowed not to watch any news for the next week. "Time to take my own advice," she said out loud to the kitchen. She placed her dishes in the dishwasher, poured herself another cup of coffee, and opened her laptop for a quick peek before she went into her meditation routine. The pain in her ankle was starting to subside.

Crystal had sent a picture of her, Orestes, and their mother eating ice cream in Las Vegas after the show. Halley texted a smiley face and then was on to other messages.

She logged into her website and was going to write a short comment in her blog, thanking the people of Los Angeles for their kindness in hosting her. Several new messages had responded to her posts from a week ago. Her topic had been the natural powers of intuition that woman possessed.

One was disturbing.

'You lead women on a path of their own destruction.'

The comment was made with the anonymous designation so Halley could not find the messenger. It had been placed there on Friday, the day she gave her presentation at the auditorium.

She wanted to write a response, but deleted it instead. She did answer and comment on several others who left complimentary kudos and thank you's. Then she wrote notes to several people who had assisted with the program and the facilities planning, including the small staff she'd hired to sell her merchandise and tickets for her upcoming Summit event. She even emailed an acknowledgement to the caterers and the florist who delivered the rose petals she always had scattered on stage as her signature. The event security staff also got a personalized note. She delivered several online payments so that all the bills for the event were paid for promptly.

By ten, there was still no message from Gibril, so she decided to begin her meditation. She lit a candle and played the background instrumental music that put her into a calm and serene place in preparation for her exercise. The large rose-colored leather chair felt delicious warming her seated frame as she closed her eyes and began opening herself to the universe.

At first, she found herself in the familiar rain forest. She noticed Gibril wasn't anywhere around. She could hear voices, but saw no one. She turned frequently, expecting to see someone approach, but she was alone with the sounds of the forest, and the muffled voices remained far enough away that the words were unclear and scrambled.

It surprised her when she called out Gibril's name and waited to hear it echo off the massive trees in the redwood forest. Then her mouth formed the beginning of Morgan's name, and she was aware she was fighting her vision, holding herself back from speaking it to the forest. She was not going to allow him back into her vision—or her life.

Before she could win the battle of wills, her ex did appear at a distance, but he turned his back, put his hands in his pockets, and slowly walked ahead of her at an easy gait she could follow. And that's what she did.

She watched him search the trees, look up to the sky, briefly glance around to make sure she was following, and then bend to pick up a stick littering the plank walkway. Halley kept her distance, but she found the way he carried his powerful body the same as she used to watch when they were married. He was a mass of muscle and physical torque waiting to explode with a silent veneer that masked the intensity inside. The familiar feeling she was safe when he was around did comfort her, though she had to work to remove the worry line now embedded between her eyes. She told herself she'd stop the vision if he came any closer to her.

And then he just disappeared into the fog of the forest. One second, he had been there, and the next, just gone. She opened her eyes and then heard the chirping of her cell phone in the kitchen.

It was Gibril. "I was wondering if you were still partying," she teased into the phone.

"I told you, not that kind of party. I was home early. I probably should have rung you up and insisted I come over."

"My shriveled body barely got itself out of the bath

in time to fall asleep in bed."

"So you still want to take that walk and have a picnic? I took the liberty of buying some things at the deli on my way home."

"I'm game. But I've twisted my ankle, so let's not make it too long a walk, okay? So, shall I meet you?"

"Will you let me through your security system? I'd like to pick you up, if you don't mind."

"I'd like that."

An HOUR LATER, Halley was sitting in Gibril's Tesla as he barreled down the winding hill toward the valley floor. His car was made to be driven hard, but the incredible silence of the electric vehicle gave her the illusion of flying. Conversations weren't drowned out by the gurgling and revving of a gasoline engine. Gibril negotiated the turns to perfection. She wondered if he'd had had any previous racing experience.

They arrived at Lytton Park situated in the hills behind the Stanford campus. The lot was nearly full, but several groups of people were packing up after an early morning bike ride, and he soon found a spot.

Gibril leaned over and surprised her with a quick kiss. "I've been thinking of doing that for three days now."

She was going to lean into him again and say something like, "Let's make it count," but Gibril was already out of the car and headed for her side to escort her out. Even the way he held her hand was chaste, delicate and careful. And it was the first time she noticed his hand trembling.

"Are you okay today, Gibril?"

He abruptly looked up from retrieving a basket from the trunk. "What kind of foolery is ruminating around your pretty little head this morning, Halley?"

"I don't know." She shrugged and watched him close the trunk with a delicate press of a button. The basket handle was slung over his forearm as he walked toward her. "You seem nervous."

Gibril gave her one of those legendary dark smiles, his perfect white teeth glowing in the sunlight of the day. "Ah, I see. Your imagination is overactive today."

"I call it intuition," Halley said with firmness.

"Whatever it is, I honor it. But the answer to your question is that I've been looking forward to spending some time with you. It's been a week already. Perhaps the anticipation of our time together?" He drew his eyebrows up and curled his lower lip down as he made the silly face.

They locked arms, and Halley pushed the thoughts out of her head as they walked through the turning leaves and lush loam that made a carpet of the park's walking trails. The smells of fall were in the air— somewhere a fire was burning, the musty smell of crumbling bark, bright green moss, and rotting under-brush was pungent and somehow welcoming in its familiarity.

Gibril took them up a gentle slope to a small mead-ow with filtered sunlight and placed the basket down at his feet. Then he spread an old bedspread out on the forest floor and motioned for her to sit down.

He served her up a plastic container with several varieties of fresh fruit, including red seedless grapes. He had slices of quiche and an artichoke frittata and showed her the dark chocolate brownies wrapped in plastic for dessert.

"This is all very nice," she said as he poured her a glass of pink sparkling champagne. "You thought of everything."

He was leaning back on his elbow, his long legs stretched perpendicular to her. His smile could set the forest on fire. "Just being here with you is enough. It would still be perfect if I'd forgotten everything!" He held up his glass, and they toasted. "To a perfect fall day, and to us."

As their glasses touched, her eyes teared up at his thoughtful attentiveness. She'd missed the little inti-mate moments that could occur between a man and a woman. And especially in this circumstance, where the two of them came from such different worlds, the apex of their affection touched her.

"I have some news that I think you will like." Gibril's voice was melodic and full of passion and mystique.

"Oh, what?"

"My niece is coming to your event. She wants to meet the famous Halley Hansen."

Halley was floored. Never had Gibril mentioned any member of his family was remotely interested in her seminars and events. And though he'd never said so, she guessed that, culturally, women in his family would usually not be interested in her message.

"That's fantastic, Gibril. She lives here in the Bay Area?"

"She wants to go to Stanford. Yes, she wants to live here." Gibril let his head bob from side to side, "But her grades may not be quite good enough. I reminded her of what you say all the time…"

"*'You never know if you don't try,'*" they both said in unison.

"How old is she?"

"She's nineteen. Very pretty. Very modern. In my culture, she's nearly an old maid. Her younger sister is getting married next summer."

"Well, I highly approve," Halley said. "You must bring her to the stage afterwards, or perhaps she can join us for dinner? And thank you for encouraging her."

"Believe me, I did very little. She bought her ticket with her own money. This is also not something we are used to in our family."

"I know. I've spoken to girls' schools about this. In some religious families, they are not allowed to handle money. I think that's backward, Gibril." She plucked a few more grapes and enjoyed their juice.

Again, the sensation crept upon her and she quickly glanced around them to see if someone was nearby, and found no one.

"You saw something?" he asked.

"I've just been having this awful feeling lately. Jitters."

"Ah, so you projected onto me the jitters in your own stomach." He winked and sipped his champagne.

He was the handsomest, most cultured man she'd ever spent time with. Even when she'd done her modeling in high school and college and her brief and tumultuous foray into acting as a young starlet in her early twenties, the male models and other people she'd worked with didn't have the dignity, the bearing, and the charisma Gibril had. His manliness was gentle and refined, and soon, she completely forgot her fear of being watched.

She finished her glass and laid it down on the spread before scooting over closer to him, leaning forward and covering his mouth with hers. The sensuous lemon scent of his smooth face and the curly dark hair she loved running her fingers through were unnecessary enhancements. In that moment, she had surrendered completely to him.

But he separated, held out his arms, and twisted her body so that they lay side by side, facing each other on the cotton fabric. His forefinger traced the length of her nose. "Do you think about what it might be like to have children, Halley?"

"Children?" She hid her surprise well since Gibril didn't react. Inside, Halley's gut was doing flip-flops.

"You must have thought about it. Most women do," he persisted, following up with a soft kiss.

This was the fork in the road where she fully grasped how she was different than *most women*— which was a term she despised. The thought had never really crossed her mind. It was something she knew would only come with the right man at her side, if at all.

"You look troubled, Halley. Have I upset you?"

"No, Gibril." She rolled over on her back and looked at the blue sky peeking between the golden canopy above. "I have never sat and longed for that day. That's not how I'm wired. I want what I'm doing *now*." She rolled back to face him again. "Does that make me a terrible person? And you should be honest with me here. This is one of those times that require complete honesty. Don't sugar-coat it."

His smile was hesitant; his eyes sparkled, but didn't match the smile. She knew she wasn't getting the truth from him. "No, my dear. I could never think of you as a terrible person. I think it's a question of timing for you."

Halley sat up and hugged her knees. Something was beginning to bother her, and she knew discretion was necessary. Her words needed to be sparse, to the point, and unflinching but not too cold. The dreamy, easy fantasy of the afternoon had dissipated somewhat.

"I think what you're saying, Gibril, is that you think someday I'll settle down and then want a family, correct?"

"Yes. Perhaps my words were unfortunate choices." He also sat up. She could see he was becoming edgy. "You are so different from all the women I've known and grown up with, Halley."

"In what way?" She still wasn't looking at his face.

"Well, in my culture—and I admit, parts of it are a throwback to some ancient times with archaic customs and beliefs—I was raised that when a woman shows you her body, she is telling you she is willing to bear you a child. Now, I don't want that to sound—"

"That sounds horrible. You don't own me just because we've slept together. You mean to say that you expect now that I'll want to have your children?"

"No. I was just asking, Halley. Musing is all." He touched her arm with his slender fingers, slid them down to her wrist, then pulled her hand toward his mouth, and gave her a tender kiss on the inside of her palm. "It is the highest form of compliment, sweet Halley. I mean this only out of the highest respect for you as a woman. Don't let your Western values cloud what could be a beautiful experience."

Halley pulled her hand away and gulped in air, trying to calm her nerves. She was nearing a flashpoint. The other thing she didn't like was that he was trying to convince her, seduce her to doing something she clearly wasn't ready for. He was very good. Very subtle. But the underlying desire in his tone of voice was unmistakable. She decided to give him a little chance to clarify, just in case she'd gotten it wrong.

"It's true, Gibril. I *am* a Western woman, raised in a different culture, but I think we share the same values of hard work, honesty, giving our most to our fellow man. You help start-up business have a future by bringing capital and opportunity they wouldn't have any other way. I bring ideas and a different way of thinking to women so they could perhaps enhance their own lives with those views. They do the work, but I give them the emotional capital. Don't you see that? We both make the world a better place, a place of opportunity and success. A bright future."

"I see that. Sure. Point well-taken. But don't you see bringing children into this world also as an opportunity?"

"You mean take them on the road during my speaking engagements or letting someone else raise them?"

"No, making a different choice for your future. A future as a mother and partner."

"And give up my business?"

"When you are ready."

Halley adjusted her legs so they pulled around her, and she looked back at Gibril, who was sitting cross-legged with his hands folded in his lap, facing her. "And would you give up your business to raise a family? Do you think that someday you'd give it all up to become a father for your children?"

Gibril smiled and examined his hands. Softly, he responded, "You've got me there, Halley. I do not think that way, at least not now."

"And that's the same as me." She could see he was struggling with her answers and the pointed question he couldn't find the proper words for. She wondered how he could not know this about her. But the truth was painfully obvious. If there was to be a future between them, Gibril would require that she change.

That just wasn't going to happen.

CHAPTER 7

MORGAN SURVEYED THE empty plates—all twelve of them. They'd ordered extra servings of sausage and eggs, along with banana, chocolate chip, raspberry, and old fashioned buttermilk pancakes when Lambert told him he was on the team—on a restricted basis.

The Commander looked green when he finally got up, grunted, made a run for the bathroom, and then returned, his color only slightly improved.

"I can't believe I did that. Damn, you frogs. I should have never accepted your invitation."

J.J. grinned, chewing on a toothpick. "You get all caught up in it, like three guys in a pissing contest. I think you won there, Commander."

"Feeding frenzy. Like on those zombie movies," added Morgan.

Lambert nearly headed for the bathroom again, but recovered enough to adjust his belt and give out a good belch. "Since I'm going to be absolutely miserable riding that transport back to Norfolk, along with God knows what kind of equipment smelling of gasoline, you two can split the tab. I'll catch you for a dinner when this thing is all done."

"Thought your office was in D.C.," Morgan asked.

"I'm stopping in Norfolk on some Navy business. I'll drive up later in the week." He presented the bill to J.J. "All yours."

Lambert picked up his bag and briefcase.

"I have some things I need to leave with you." He leaned forward, craning his neck to peer down the hallway. "They still have that old phone room in the back?"

"They sure do," said J.J.

"I'll lead the way." Morgan waved at a couple former Team guys from his group as they filed into the storage room. Off to the side was the padded phone room of WWII vintage that used to house four payphones. Numbers written on the wall were still four figure ones preceded by a name of a street or monument. The devices were long gone, but the door was still intact, so Lambert motioned for them to get inside, and he shut the collapsing plexiglass frame behind them.

He pulled a large manila envelope out from his briefcase, placing it on the scratched metal shelf of the old booth. "This is the rest of the information on the mission. You look it over. If you have any questions, don't call me on your personal phones. We use this." He handed J.J. a box containing a brand new cell phone kit. "It's a burner. I suggest you guys get another one for you to use, Hansen. You can program this one to use up to ten phone lines at once, which you can delete at any time and keep reusing. Use the blocking feature for calling anyone but my office, understood?"

Both Morgan and J.J. agreed.

"And you call this number to report. Don't put it into auto-dial, and don't carry this card. You memorize it." He handed the two of them each his Department of the Navy card, showing his retired designation. "On the back, I've written my personal cell. Only in an emergency. We do all our talking on your burner, and we need an update as often as is necessary. You want more assets, someone who's a specialist, you let me know."

"How will you contact us?" J.J. asked.

"You check in with me. That's how it works. I'm not supposed to be running this show, you are. I'm not supposed to even know anything about it. But I want your information regular, just like diarrhea. The more information the better. You got anything I need to run down, let me know."

Morgan flipped open the envelope and noticed it was stuffed with papers, clippings, and photographs.

"Don't go looking at that anywhere but in private. You lock it up with your long guns in your safe stash. I assume you both still have one?"

It was a dumb question.

"My personal opinion is that they're planning this thing carefully, and unlike some of my co-workers, I think they'll wait for the big event to pull this off. Something showy. Your gal there, Hansen, has a huge program scheduled for about three weeks' time, and all the information is in it, including a couple of tickets to the event. Our team thinks that's what they'll do. So you have to get your ducks in order, and you don't have a lot of time."

Next, he handed J.J. a credit card, pulled from inside the wallet in his breast pocket. "I'll fill this up when necessary. I don't want you using anything of your own, unless it's something you'd do on the outside. Everything has to be done on this card. The Pin on the card for cash withdrawals is set to the last four of your social, Johnson"

"Thanks." J.J. slipped the card into his wallet.

"I've got five thousand in cash in an envelope in here, so don't lose it. Hansen, you run everything expense-wise through Johnson"

"Will do."

Next, he handed J.J. a new California driver's license. "From now on, you'll be Hank Forsburg. That's the address we'll send things to you, an opened mailbox downtown, one of the CIA assets. It can also be used as a place to drop off messages and things we need you to get to us right away. And it's secure." He turned to address Morgan. "You, my friend, are going to remain Morgan Hansen for now. Nothing changes for you. Johnson will be assigned an apartment we've cleared for him, but he should stay with you for starters. That's all being arranged as we speak. I'll get you a key to that apartment later on."

"Wait a minute, Commander. I've got a wife and kids," J.J. moaned. "I can't leave them alone. I can take a leave at the school, no problem there, but my family needs me."

"You have to consider this a deployment. You're going undercover. You'll grow out your hair, a beard, too. Same for you, Hansen."

J.J. was still shaking his head.

"Look, chances are this mission won't last more than a few weeks, but we don't know for sure. Consider yourself deployed, just in your own country this time. It has to be done that way, for your family's protection. We don't want any of your old buddies or friends or family to recognize you on the street or hang around to become persons they can follow to get to you guys, understood?"

The stuffy room enhanced the spirit of danger that

lingered after Lambert finished talking. The Commander opened the accordion door, and a burst of fresh air greeted them. J.J. and Morgan said their goodbyes. Lambert wished them well.

As they watched the patriot wind his way through the Scupper and outside to the street, Morgan knew the man was wondering if he'd made the biggest mistake of his life. He'd work hard to prove Lambert's trust was well-placed.

He was back on a team! Suddenly, everything around him brightened.

THE TWO FORMER SEALs returned to Morgan's house to go over the envelope of material Lambert had given them. Inside, they found glossy photographs of Halley as a model and photos of her sitting beside Morgan in his dress whites at a SEAL Foundation function. Her radiant complexion and award-winning smile stunned everyone around her in the receiving line. Morgan remembered that night, when all was well with them. Just a few storm clouds on the horizon in those days.

Whoever had gathered these pictures had better be from the government side of the ledger, he thought. Otherwise, there was a traitor in the Brotherhood, and that wasn't very likely. But he had seen pictures like these posted on walls in the Team 3 building and suspected there had been no foul play.

But when he turned one over, he saw the unmistakable Arabic writing, and his blood turned to ice.

"Damn!" J.J. whispered. "How the hell did they get these?"

"Could have been someone who tossed them out during a relocation or a divorce. You know how it goes. They could have picked it up in the trash."

"Do you think they've been collecting these all this time? These are over ten years old."

"That's a fact."

Morgan read several dossiers on key members of an Al-Qaeda cell and training camp operating out of a radical mosque in Stockton, California. The report indicated that several clerics in a row there had been deported for irregularities with their tax returns. The current Imam, Mohammad Al-Moustafa, was able to successfully negotiate the learning curve and had kept his record clean. But he'd been known to preach certain extremist ideologies, the report said.

Morgan looked at the photograph of the handsome Imam. His beard was well-trimmed and his eyebrows plucked and professionally shaped. A newspaper clipping quoted him as stating he was a reformist who believed in women's rights.

I believe there should be bridges between our diverse communities and gender equality for all. We should seek to enhance our education by teaching tolerance, peace, and love for all mankind. I condemn terrorism, the pamphlet said.

The dossier stated they did not know his real country of origin, only that he had spent his early years in the Middle East somewhere, and had never traveled abroad before settling in central California. He was a very active blogger and savvy with social media.

Other members of the cleric's mosque were researched, some with or without photographs. The mosque and the Imam's private quarters were requested to be wiretapped, but the case was denied by a San Francisco judge.

When he came upon the picture of Halley holding hands with a slender Middle Eastern-looking man, Morgan's blood pressure exploded. He turned over the photograph, and it had been date stamped from a month ago, taken in Palo Alto. Beneath the date was written *Gibril Messi, boyfriend, age 36.*

Morgan frantically searched through the reports, looking for a write-up on Messi.

"Here you go," announced J.J., who handed him a single-page biography on the man, with several newspaper clippings attached.

Gibril Messi of Saratoga, California.

Family of Origin: Stated on H1B Visa form as Sudan, but application for citizenship states United Arab Emirates as family's home address.

Sponsored by Focus Forum, a venture capitalist firm located in San Jose. He has one year remaining on the visa, pending his citizenship application. He is eligible for another three-year extension.

Messi has two sisters also living in Silicon Valley, who are married with children who are U.S. citizens. Several uncles and cousins reside in Modesto, California and maintain a large family farm, with another family branch in farming in Loomis, California.

Morgan knotted his eyebrows. "Where the hell is Loomis?"

"Sacramento. North and east of Sacramento."

"And Modesto is the central valley."

J.J. scratched his head. "More north, but it's beyond the East Bay. Big farming community, like Loomis."

"Thanks, man." Morgan continued reading.

Attempts to interview neighbors or sponsoring company, given the time constraints, were not possible.

The attached cutouts from the Palo Alto Times showed Messi and some of the other junior partners at Focus Forum announcing their successful investment in the startup firm, Cardiowise. The article went on to report the firm had developed a new form of heart monitoring, spearheaded by two physicians from Stanford.

Also attached were newspaper clippings from society functions, Messi standing in a group with various other Silicon Valley icons, occasionally with women at his side.

"Anything of interest?" J.J. was still searching for more on Messi.

"Just background. They don't have the family on a watch list or flagged, so it all looks pretty legit. I think Halley would be a fairly good judge of character, but then she picked me, didn't she?" Morgan dropped the page and began searching through other files.

"Which shows she is a very good judge of character, I'd say," J.J. responded.

There were translations from Arabic of phone conversations which specifically mentioned Halley Hansen and her Success Summit organization. Links to videos on YouTube featuring Halley's gatherings were referenced. Photos of the large crowd of mostly women in the audience were frequent. Several articles touted her seminars as the "largest gathering of women in the United States."

Morgan began to get increasingly agitated, reading over the material and learning about this group, which didn't appear to have anything to do with the boyfriend or his family. He was sure the intel was completely accurate.

"J.J., first thing we do is find out who is running her security. I want to know how much experience they've had, how they handle the crowds, and whether or not the venues are properly swept, vetted, and secured."

"No kidding. I'm willing to bet she has no idea all this focus is on her."

Morgan agreed. "Just not sure what approach to take. With Halley, you don't bullshit your way in. She has to be told the truth. And then she might reject it. That's going to be the hardest part."

"So a visit is in order. You want me to do it first, alone? I mean, would she distrust the information if she knew it was partially coming from you?"

"She might. Lambert didn't say she was to be left in the dark, did he?"

"Oh God, no. The opposite. She has to be told, and she has to cooperate with us. And if it's too risky, just my opinion here, her big event should be cancelled." J.J.'s pained look told Morgan he didn't want to have that conversation with the unflappable Halley Hansen.

"And if we interview her security team, we need not to tip them off we're looking for cell sympathizers or outright members. But I'm betting someone close to her is somehow connected to this Imam."

J.J. read out loud a note stating he was authorized to use lethal force if he was forced to, either in defense of himself, other members of their team, the subject, or the innocents around her. "They're asking for a laundry list of what firepower we prefer, too, Hansen."

"Like Christmas, isn't it, J.J.?"

"Hell yeah. I'm going to have to do some practicing on the range. Been about three years since I held a handgun."

Morgan had never let a month go by without sharpening his training. He'd qualified Expert and didn't ever intend on losing that skill level.

They reviewed the remainder of reports and clippings, studying diagrams and photographs. Morgan handed J.J. the cash. Everything was spread out over Morgan's kitchen table as he scanned the large trove of material. The nerds had done a good job. They had lots of trails of evidence to follow-up.

Just like they'd done on the Teams, the two of them began to build a strategy and discover the holes so they could plug them.

"We need an interpreter and someone we trust to go inside the Mosque," said J.J.

"Jackie Daniels still around San Diego? You think he could do it?"

The Iraqi interpreter had worked with SEAL Team 3 for several years before he and his family were allowed to immigrate to the San Diego area. The man was responsible for saving hundreds of American troops lives over his years of service.

"Or he knows someone else we can trust," answered J.J.

"I'm gonna give Kyle Lansdowne a call. He'd know. Hopefully, no one will recognize him in Stockton."

J.J. agreed with the request.

They spent the rest of the day working out details and making lists of things they'd be submitting to Lambert. J.J. was going home to spend one last night with the family. If the apartment wasn't forthcoming, he'd bunk with Morgan temporarily.

But right away, there was going to be one major fork in the road. That concerned Halley's help. Morgan thought it was a toss-up whether or not she'd agree to cooperate. She was wicked smart, he admitted, but she didn't always take the smart path. So it was incumbent on him to speak with her in the only way he knew how to: honestly and without any sugarcoating.

Morgan felt like the old days, when he'd be preparing with his Teammates for some mission. They didn't have the time to rehearse every scenario, and they were without the rest of the squad they usually used, a twelve-man unit, but it was still thrilling to be in the fight once again. His government was counting on him. J.J. would be counting on him. Halley would be counting on him.

He worried for Halley's safety, but he worried more for what her reaction would be when she saw him for the first time in nearly ten years. He was determined to complete the mission successfully, no matter what she said or did. He knew he could handle anything she could dish out.

CHAPTER 8

CRYSTAL CORTEZ REPORTED for work on Monday morning at eight. Halley was already at her desk. She brought in a large bouquet of red roses that had been left outside the second gate. Halley was shocked.

The long-stemmed beauties had a note attached. Halley's fingers fumbled with the little envelope until she pulled out the card. Crystal set the bouquet on her desk and waited for further instruction.

Thank you for yesterday. –Gibril.

"I think I know who those are from, unless you've picked up another admirer," teased Crystal.

"You'd be right."

"He's such a gentleman, and he's not difficult to look at, either."

Halley sighed and sat back down at her desk. "I think we should put these in the living room on the coffee table. Add some water, too. I've got so much paperwork here, I'm afraid I'll upend them."

"You got it, boss." Crystal removed the lovely roses and came back seconds later. "I got your numbers this morning online. I need to confirm it with the staff at the Grand Fordham when they open, but I think we're sold out! Congratulations!"

"Seriously? We've got two thousand four hundred ticket sales?"

"That many entries at least. Assuming all their credit cards go through. The Fordham staff said that nearly thirty percent of the sales for these things happen the last two to three days of the event, so you're way ahead of the game. I think, at this rate, you'll be wanting to do another Hero Summit in Hawaii later in the year next year."

"Wouldn't that be wonderful?"

The two women had a brief meeting. Halley asked her to get the link to the television interview from the Santa Monica station. They went down their list of things for the Summit event in three weeks. Halley still had to redo some of her material from last year's event and she crossed out two days this week for her total emersion into those notes.

There was a buzz at the front gate, and Crystal went to go answer it. Visitors rarely dropped by unannounced, so Halley was curious. She checked her phone and hadn't gotten a message from Gibril, so she texted him, bending her rules somewhat. The roses were beautiful, after all, and the perfect way to start her work week.

The roses are stunning. You shouldn't have.

Gibril answered back immediately. *As stunning as you are. I love your honesty. Just wanted you to know I'm still here.*

Halley was pleased Gibril had taken her comments yesterday so well. They'd cut short their little romantic picnic, and it was an awkward drive home, but she realized it would be better to talk about it later, after they both had had time to think. Otherwise, she could find herself saying things she might regret. But standing her ground and letting him know where she was about the whole marriage and children scenario was important. If they ever could develop into something longer-lasting, it had to be based on trust and truth.

The roses were a nice way of telling her she was still valued. Indeed, he'd said as much when they parted. This underscored it.

Halley answered him back. *You know how I love to be spoiled. Thank you for cheering up my Monday. I, too, enjoyed our talk. I'm glad my—"* She erased the last part, because it would have been a lie to say she worried he'd take it the wrong way. She replaced that phrase with, *Nice that our friendship can withstand honest talk.*

Indeed. I'll call you later tonight?

Sure.

Crystal entered the office looking perplexed. "You aren't going to believe this, but your ex-husband is at the gate wanting to talk to you. Did you know about this?"

"Of course not!" Halley's pulse soared, and she felt her chest go blotchy with a genuine flush. All of a sudden, she couldn't think straight. She stood. Then she sat. Then she looked up to Crystal and asked, "What does he want?"

Crystal shrugged. "He just says he has some important things to discuss with you. He said it was personal. Sorry."

Halley tried to recall if he'd left her an email or message stating he needed to get together, but came up blank. It wouldn't hurt to talk to him, of course, but it was so unexpected, clear out of the blue after over ten years, that she didn't know how to trust it.

"Let's buzz him in. I don't think he's been here before, so be sure to give him instructions to the second gate."

"You got it."

Halley found herself dashing to the bathroom to check on her appearance. She was casual when she worked from home, wearing a warm cashmere sweater and some wool slacks. Thank God today wasn't one of those where she worked in her sweats all day. She combed her hair and applied more lip gloss.

She removed her wool slippers and replaced them with her heels, tucked discretely under her desk. Then she walked to the foyer to await his entrance.

She saw the massive shadow cross the stained glass side panels of her front door before she heard the knock. Crystal had retired to the office and closed the door to give them privacy, so now Halley found herself gripping the antique brass door handle as if it was keeping her on her feet. Suddenly, she was standing in front of Morgan's warrior body. His shoulders were even bigger than when they'd been married, and his waist was narrower. He was in the best shape of his life. His bright blue eyes saw right through the cool façade she was desperately trying to display.

It was when he looked her body down and then back up very slowly without expression that got to her. She felt naked and began to shake. That old familiar tingle traveled down her spine, the little needles extending up the back of her neck, making the skin super tender there. She inhaled, held her stomach in, and greeted him.

"Welcome, Morgan. I don't think you've been here before."

She stepped aside, giving him a wide berth to enter. Closing the oak door behind him, Halley placed both hands on the grained wood and turned, her back smashed against the oak, bracing for what he'd say next.

"No. This is nice. You've done well, Halley. Very impressive." Morgan was once again examining her white cashmere sweater and she suspected he'd grown a hard-on, because that always happened when he was excited about something. She was not going to allow herself to check, no matter how curious she was.

Her business persona showed up just in time to rescue her unexpected jitters. "Can I offer you something? Water, coffee, or tea?"

"You drink coffee?"

She smiled. "I still have a cup or two every morning. The one habit I couldn't shake."

His eyes roamed over the fuzzy sweater again, and then he adjusted quickly, all business. "I'll have coffee. Cream if you have it."

"I have half and half."

"Perfect."

He followed her into the kitchen, examining the cabinet detail and admiring the tall ceilings and granite countertops.

Halley brewed them both a specialty grind she imported from Hawaii, stopping by the refrigerator to put a teaspoon of cream in her own cup and a tablespoon in Morgan's. "I think I got it right, but you let me know," she said as she handed him the mug. "Now, what's this all about? Should we sit at the table or would you prefer the living room?"

He opted for the living room, settling behind the bouquet of roses so she took the loveseat to his right. She placed two coasters beside him so they could both share the little side table in the corner.

"First, I have to tell you this isn't a social call. I really should have been in touch over the years, but, well, things were so nasty, I decided to just let us both retire permanently to our corners. But I have come across some information I think you need to know about." He squirmed, leaning forward, his mug balanced between his scarred and thick fingers. He was the only person she knew who could make a huge Coffee Company mug look small.

Halley soon noticed he appeared uncomfortable in a pair of slacks and a button-down long sleeved shirt, instead of the canvas slip-ons and cargo pants with some politically irreverent tee shirt he was used to. The collar was open, revealing a clean white tee shirt beneath. The button-down was freshly laundered, perhaps new, but the pants weren't. And he'd made a point of polishing a pair of brown shoes he owned when they were married.

Morgan never wore aftershave, but his manscent was pleasant and easy to inhale.

"Go ahead, Morgan. I'm not a China doll. I can take whatever you have to tell me."

He took another sip from his coffee, carefully placed it on the coaster provided, and asked, "Can your friend hear us? I have to be sure this conversation is private."

She stared at the closed office door. "She wouldn't—"

"Then turn on some music, something in the background so she can't. You have any listening devices in here?"

Halley was shocked. Wrinkling up her nose, she answered him, "No! Most certainly not!"

He was composed, drew more coffee from the steaming cup, and waited until she had turned on her satellite radio to a New Age station and returned to the love seat.

Morgan looked her straight in the eyes. "Halley, you're in danger. Grave danger. I know you want the straight truth, so I'm going to give it to you without embellishment. We've uncovered a terrorist plot against you, and we think it's going to happen at your Success Summit in a couple of weeks."

Halley blinked nearly a dozen times before Morgan's words sunk in.

"Terrorist plot? How did you find out about this?"

"I've been tasked to work on this, to give you protection. What we actually want to do is catch these guys, but we mainly want to stop the tragedy from happening."

"I didn't know you were still in the Navy. I thought—"

"I'm doing something different. This is a one-project thing. You remember Jay Johnson? Former Teammate? We're working on this together."

"But how did they find out—who is in charge of this-this investigation?" She was having trouble grasping why anyone would want to sabotage her event, attack women who were trying to improve their lives.

"Now that they've lost their caliphate, they are turning up the heat on their assets here in the U.S. They're looking for ways to make a big, showy statement. Like 9/11."

Halley saw in his eyes the hurt and pain she'd never seen before. "You mean Al-Queda? Is that who you're speaking of? And, Morgan, do you have proof of this?"

"Yes, and I'm afraid we do."

"Show me."

"Well, hon—" He stopped himself, and she saw the brief shade of red that covered his face and then was gone in a flash. "Halley, I didn't bring all that with me, but I can arrange to show you in a safe place. What we're doing is strictly top secret, and to be effective, it has to remain that way. That's why we need your support, your agreement to cooperate fully with our team. I know it's damn awkward, me just showing up out of the blue, but this thing's for real, Halley. If you can, I'd like you to trust me."

He looked uncomfortable, all dressed up, and she knew it was for her benefit. The awkwardness of the polite chit-chat, white furniture, and the big bouquet of roses that were hard to miss were truly things outside his comfort zone. There was a sadness about him. The bravado and edge to his personality he had when he was on the Teams, that stubborn *automatic-fire* anger that she hated was not evident today. She knew enough about him to understand, though, all those things were still there, just under the surface. His calmness didn't fool her one bit. She wasn't sure she could trust him at all.

She'd been studying him rubbing his big, callused hands together nervously, fiddling with his socks, and adjusting his shoes like they were just as uncomfortable as he was sitting in her living room. Then he looked up at her, and for just a second, there was no filter to his blue eyes. A part of him was permanently damaged. At the same time, Halley understood full well she was not the healer. She was not what he needed.

But he wanted to defend something. Right now, that something was her.

"I never expected to have a calm conversation with

you again. I was so filled with rage—" she began.

"Why do you think I stayed away all those years?" This time, Morgan didn't allow his eyes to wander down her chest.

"I'm not saying I'm willing to have my life overturned by some witch hunt, and likewise, I don't want to play a part in a disaster movie. I did all the screaming I wanted to when we were married."

His crooked grin was very attractive and, for a second, caught her off guard.

"I did watch one of your movies. I have to be honest with you, Halley. The movie was terrible, but your scream was very realistic, and I should know."

She flinched at first with his backhanded compliment, but quickly got hold of herself, as it was something everyone agreed on.

"Whomever got you to the theater, I supposed you punished them severely?"

He rolled his shoulders. "I was drunk."

There it was, the excuse he always clung to. She used to think his drinking was to make her mad, but after studying more about alcoholism, she understood the addictive nature of it and that it had started from him dosing himself to oblivion so he could forget some of the aspects of his job. She wondered if that still worked for him, because it hadn't worked back then.

"Are you saying that this threat, if you can demonstrate it's real, might require that I cancel my Success Summit?"

"It's a possibility. If all else fails and we can't stop it any other way, then that would be our only option. We can't let the attack happen, regardless of whether or not you feel the threat is real enough. We can't have your innocent worshipers caught in the middle of something we could stop from occurring."

Halley reared back and felt her stomach rumble. Her jaw set tight. Her reaction to the look in his eyes when he said "worshipers" was a small measure of that sarcastic asshole she'd had enough of. It didn't take him long before he showed her.

"That's offensive. I don't have worshipers any more than you did with your bimbos at the bars in Coronado."

"Those weren't worshipers. You're right. They were Frog Hogs. But I wouldn't want to see any innocent loss of life—"

"And if I didn't agree, you'd shut the event down? That could ruin me. I'm going to need more than a hunch. Or are you going to go all commando and interfere with my life like the wrecking ball you were ten years ago? I mean, do I even have a choice?"

She knew she'd hit a nerve when Morgan stood, his hands made into fists. "I can't believe you'd want to even consider giving these terrorists a chance to make that kind of a statement. And under the guise of a financial loss? Do you even care for any of those people? Don't you feel responsible, that you could keep them safe? Wouldn't that in itself be worth it?"

The veins at the side of his neck stuck out, and his nostrils flared. He was getting dangerous. Halley carefully stood, hating the feeling he was more powerful physically and that he'd always be so. If he wanted to hurt her, he could. Trust? Was he asking her to trust him? With this kind of display?

"I think you should go."

Morgan walked around the coffee table, accidentally hitting his lower leg on the corner. Water spilled from the wide-mouth vase the roses were housed in. The container wobbled back and forth a few times, but settled without tipping over. For a second, it had stopped his forward movement. Then he resumed his beeline path to the front door.

He put his hand on the brass fixture and turned. "Just out of curiosity, if J.J. had had this little talk with you, would it have made any difference?"

"No a speck."

"I thought so." He opened the door and began to step outside.

"Morgan," she called out, not sure he could hear her.

He faced her again, leaving the doorway clear for a

speedy exit.

"I know it took a lot to come here today. I am not questioning your motives. Please understand those are not the issue. But I'm wondering if you're the right person to handle this scenario, this news of death and destruction. Perhaps there's too much history between us and it could fog everything, affect those important decisions."

Morgan's smirk showed how much pain he was in. Tilting his body so that his weight came over to one hip, probably his good one, he asked her something that she'd think about all night long. "Do you honestly think I'd ever let anything hurt you if I was alive to stop it? Do you think anyone else—your rich boyfriend or your helpers—would do the same for you?"

Just before he closed the door behind him, Morgan added, "I'll have Jay Johnson call you later on. Until then, please don't discuss any of this with anyone else or it will complicate the situation. And, Halley, if you absolutely never want to see me again, I can make that happen. Not to worry."

He closed the door, and as he did so, her eyes filled with tears.

CHAPTER 9

T HE LATE EVENING drive up and overnight stay in the cheap motel to see his ex had been a total waste of his time.

What the hell was I expecting?

He stopped for the fill-up he should have gotten when he got off the freeway in Palo Alto, grabbed a bottle of water, and sped out of town heading back to Coronado. If she took five minutes, changed her mind, and called him, he'd be nearly to Bakersfield.

Of course, she didn't have his cell number anymore. He was fairly sure of that.

Good. Let her stew.

Her lack of trust drove him up the wall. He knew trust was something that had to be earned. But people had to trust someone before that trust could be broken, and if she would never give him a chance, how could he help her? He was furious with himself for believing she would give him that opportunity. Or that she wanted his help in the first place.

If the roles were reversed, I'd give you—Morgan suddenly discovered another reason for his anger. While he trusted her to be civil, to be reasonable and logical, she didn't trust him at all. He'd had ten years to think about all the things that could have been different—he could have not taken that short deployment with SEAL Team 6 that broke his pelvis and upper femur. He could still be an active SEAL, not an aging superhero trying to relive the glory days of his twenties.

If they'd not had that argument which caused him to volunteer for that dangerous mission. *If* he hadn't been so distracted by anger on that jump and paid more attention. *If* he hadn't gotten so drunk at J.J.'s bachelor party and had those photos with the stripper leaked all over the community. If—all those ifs were adding up.

He'd relived each and every bad decision he'd made over those ten years. And, finally, he came to grips with it. He was throwing away everything meaningful in his life because suddenly he was afraid he wasn't worth it. And all he could do was watch it all piss away into nothingness. Like trying to hold together a bowl of potato chips without the bowl.

But Halley had spent the last ten years working on her business—something she'd wanted to do since the first date and they talked about her becoming a professional speaker. It was a natural segue from her modeling and miniscule acting career.

She hadn't ruminated over everything like he had. She'd just moved on. He should have done that. But she had something to look forward to building, and Morgan didn't. He was still thinking his life was over because he'd messed up his choices.

Of course, he'd made a lot of good decisions, too, but those looked little in comparison. The bad ones were looming huge.

He dialed J.J. and left him a message, using the burner phone. J.J. would not be pleased with him. Well, fuck it. Maybe Halley was right. Maybe he wasn't the man for the job. But at this point, it was too late. He wasn't a quitter, and he wasn't going to take on the first real job of his life since the Teams, something made for him, and walk away from it without trying. He hoped J.J. would have more luck. Given the chance, he knew he could prove he was the absolute best person for this mission. But he had to get past his stubborn ex-wife first. The rest was probably not going to be a piece of cake, but nothing compared to the issue of Halley and her acceptance of their help.

Damn.

His new phone beeped, surprising him.

"Didn't go that well, then?" J.J. blurted out.

"Nah. I think you'll have to bring in the cavalry.

She needs proof, and I didn't bring any of that stuff. I didn't think I had to."

"So you get your butt down here and see if you can maybe find us an interpreter or inside man. I've wrapped up here with the kids, and I'm hunkered down at your place. We'll give her a day to stew, and then perhaps she'll rethink it. If so, we can get her cooperation."

"Dayam, J.J. Am I that rusty? I used to get her to dance naked for me at the beach, even when some others might be looking over. We made love in so many public places—she trusted me, even dared me to go a couple of steps beyond. We were always pushing our boundaries over and over again. I thought some of that was still there and she could take a little risk, especially if it meant saving people who held her in such high esteem."

"She's gotten used to building an empire, sport. You challenged that. I never tell my wife how to garden or dress the kids. Never. That's her turf. If I told her she was going to have to follow my rules, well, I'd be at one of your bachelor parties, drinking beer like the rest of you. Women get this idea in their heads they can do something better than anybody else, and no one—not God, their grandmother, or their kids—can talk them out of it. They protect that like their life depends on it. That's why the female of the species is always deadliest when she's protecting her own."

"Well, maybe her life does depend on it then." Morgan's voice faded into the phone. J.J. asked him to repeat and he waved him off. "I'll be back in about seven hours. I'll try to get hold of Kyle along the way."

"Okay. Just focus on getting back here. You want to give me advice about Plan B anytime soon?"

"Shut the fuck up."

"And you said Halley was stubborn. Be safe, my man." J.J. hung up.

Morgan kept seeing the image of the man walking with Halley, hand in hand. She looked soft and happy, full of smiles. The angle of her head and the expression on her lips—well, he knew what she looked like when she was aroused.

What are you doing, man?

He halfway resigned himself to the fact that maybe he'd have this hole in his heart, that place that was raw and bloody, and it would never heal.

At least I'm alive and I'm whole. Who was he to feel sorry for himself? Other guys had it far worse than he did. Some were brain damaged, sported artificial limbs. Some were on so many pain meds that they didn't even have a life anymore. That would be hard, seeing a wife and children distance themselves, one by one, while he slowly tried to seek the sanity and wellness that would never come. At least his injury and the chip on his shoulder resulting from it would never show.

Several hours later, Lt. Kyle Lansdowne, the Team Leader of their old squad at SEAL Team 3, returned his call.

"Howz it hanging, Hansen? I was told you don't even limp anymore," Kyle said by way of greeting.

Morgan forgot about that one. It was true. The pain was gone, the hip was replaced, and for the next ten years, unless he started jumping out of airplanes again, he'd be good to go.

"Thanks, Lannie. I'm good. Staying fit, and I got a new gig I'm kind of excited about, but I'm afraid I can't talk to you about it."

"Is this some super secret shit they recruited you for in D.C.? With spooks and nerds and such?"

Of course Kyle would learn about the Division through some whispered word-of-mouth. He kept tabs on all his guys, active or not. And since Lambert had revealed they weren't in general hiring guys who had been out ten years—mostly fresh wash-outs in their prime except for some injury that disqualified them—he'd learn a lot about it happening. Morgan suspected that if there were only twelve chosen men—thirteen, if he could be counted—it was a special deal to be chosen. Who could keep their mouth shut about something like this? Especially to your old LPO?

"I'd have to say if I told you I'd have to kill you. But

your instincts are good."

"Glad to see they value your service and your physical condition, Hansen. You should be proud of that. I know I am. And I much prefer hearing about you doing something important than conducting meetings at the Scupper for orphaned husbands, if you get my drift."

No wonder Lambert didn't have much respect for him. All of a sudden, the little Bone Frog Brotherhood shit looked stupid, like a coffee klatch or knitting club. Nothing like doing something really important to reveal what you'd been doing wasn't.

"Called self-preservation. I don't get the well ones, that's for sure. You have to be a bit damaged to have a group leader like me."

"You deprecate yourself too much. Give credit where it's due. You've survived the last ten years, and I understand you don't have that vacant stare I see all too often. When you're ready to put down your boots, you might consider becoming a counselor. I think you'd make one hell of one."

Morgan didn't want to go that far. He needed to change the subject right away. "So, Lannie, we need an interpreter, someone who can go infiltrate a certain closed society. Perhaps blend in and look like a whack job."

"Does he have to be native? They're turning out

tons of high quality guys from the language schools these days."

"I was wondering about Jackie Daniels."

"Not sure he's available. He's being recruited heavily by private industry. The family might be moving."

"That's a shame."

"I got a couple of good recommendations for a couple of guys who could play the part of a recent radical recruit. Would that interest you at all?"

"Are they done?"

"These two couldn't make the last qualifier. Eyesight issues and something else medical. Got them all the way to workup and decided they had to be scratched. A damn shame, too."

"That would bite. Do they look Middle Eastern at all?"

"Hell no. They both are carrot tops, and they sunburn faster than a snowflake melts. No way to pass for Middle Eastern, but they got the language and culture down. They're a hell of an asset, in my opinion. And they need a job right quick, too."

"Okay, can I stop by tonight if I'm back early enough or tomorrow to get their information? Would you vouch for me?"

"How much you want me to say?"

"Nothing at all about the mission. You don't know anything. I gotta get permission for the new hire or hires. Their skills are good, like can they shoot?"

"Qualified expert first time through. Avid hunters. They can track and shoot with anything manual or automatic. Survival training top notch. One's tall and the other one is like his alter ego, short and stubby. But they became friends in BUD/s, and it's kind of ironic they washed out together, too. I'd take the pair."

"Okay, so you tell them we need interpreters for a special diplomatic mission, then."

"Like an overseas gig. For some reason I was thinking this was about the Homeland."

"You didn't hear that from me. Just tell them that. I can meet with them tomorrow if I get the approval tonight."

"You got it." Kyle was on his way to signing off when he hesitated, asking Morgan about Halley. "Christy tells me she's seen her all over the T.V. lately. She's got quite an empire going. Good for her. You must be proud."

"Yeah, except we're divorced. You know that, right?"

"Of course I do. I hope I didn't bring up something painful."

"No more painful than stepping in a bear trap barefoot, Kyle. But I'll live. You take care and give Christy a long, lingering kiss with some tongue action."

"It would be my pleasure. Later, kid."

Morgan made a mental note to be in more contact with his former LPO. Talking the shit was good for his psyche. It was a whole lot more healing than dwelling about things that could have been and now never could be or watching the Frog Hogs at the Scupper trying to pick up the younger guys, not the second time losers.

His whole world view had changed in the past two days. For the better. For the first time, he felt in his bones that he could actually pull this off.

CHAPTER 10

H ALLEY WAS DISTRACTED most of the day, and the longer it went on, the angrier she became. The information Morgan had laid on her caused her to doubt everyone she worked with, even Crystal. She worried about her conversations being taped, wondered if there were cameras in her bathroom, her bedroom. She wondered about the mechanic who would be fixing her car and the landscapers who had the double gate codes and came every week. Her housekeeper, who barely spoke English, could have been an enemy spy. Her driver. Orestes.

How unfair it had been of him to just come in and poop on her life and then leave. Well, yes, she did offend him, but he'd offended her first. It was a pattern she'd grown to despise when they were married. He'd be gone. After he'd come home, he would turn her orderly world into complete chaos with no regard for her or her routine and just as she was getting used to it, he'd be off again playing with the boys. It was as though she was raising a teenager, but a huge and lethal one. She'd had ten years of working on herself, but this one man could still walk through her door and upset her whole world with just a few little words. Would she ever feel safe again on stage?

And how horrible it would be if there were nothing to this, that it had been a mistake, a hoax, or false alarm? Her serenity and ease with her events was shattered. No way could this genie be put back into the bottle. All the cows were loose from the barn and running all over the freeway of her life. She was miserable.

The worst thing was that she had no one to talk to unless she broke the rules. And who would know more about terrorist plots than Gibril? But would he be offended if she brought this up to him?

There you go again. You're not supposed to worry about what they think of you. That's none of your business.

Though she'd said it hundreds of times, perhaps thousands of times now, that little statement seemed trite and silly in the face of all the danger that could be lurking ahead. This was real stuff. This was life and death. This was what happened when she brushed up against Morgan's world. It would spill over and infect her.

The thought of cancelling the event was unthinkable, yet Morgan had been right. The health and safety of those women who paid good money to hear her words of wisdom was what was important, not the monetary loss. Yes, it had taken her years to get to this point financially. But nobody said life came with a guarantee. What she earned could be swept away in the blink of an eye. The country could be embroiled in war. She could get sick.

Enough! I'm horrible at taking my own advice. The worst.

Crystal had been looking at her sideways all afternoon. On a couple of occasions, she found herself snapping at her, especially when she made a cheery response. Halley didn't want to do chitchat or cheery. Then Crystal asked her a question that set her off and nearly out of control.

"So are you going to properly thank the handsome Mr. Messi for those lovely flowers?" She pretended to blush and fan herself with the papers she was holding.

Halley threw down her pen. "Dammit, Crystal. Sometimes I think you get too far into my personal life. Remember, although I enjoy working with you, we are not family, and you have no right to the information about what I do in my personal time."

She saw the tears form in Crystal's eyes as she excused herself to the restroom. Halley dropped her head on top of the sheaf of papers on her desk and covered her hair with her hands and arms. She willed the tears to come, but she was so confused and fearful, her eyes remained cold and dry. She was still seeing mangled bodies on the sidewalk and street in Portland and focusing on a vision at the Grand Fordham if a bomb leveled the whole place.

She even saw the rose petals falling last over all the ash and carnage.

Stop it. Stop it!

If it was a mind game, Morgan had pulled it off flawlessly.

Crystal came back into the office, her eyes downcast, and sat very quietly at her desk.

"I'm sorry, Crystal. I truly am."

"That's okay, Mrs. Hansen," she answered without looking up.

It broke Halley's heart to see the change that had come over her once cheerful assistant.

"Don't call me Mrs. Hansen. I'm not married. I like to be called Halley. When they arrest me, they can call me Mrs. Hansen then." She watched her assistant for signs of her cold façade melting, but found none. Even the joke wasn't going to work with her.

"Okay, let's do this, Crystal. I need to work on some things tonight, so why don't you just take the afternoon off, and we'll start all over again tomorrow.

How does that sound?"

Crystal kept her eyes low, quietly picked up her purse, and left the room without making eye contact.

Halley hoped that she'd be back tomorrow, but years of experience told her that perhaps Crystal had gone over the bend. Something between them had been lost. She just didn't have the energy to repair it today, but tomorrow was another day, and she'd do the right thing and make sure Crystal understood how valuable she had been to Halley over these past six months. It was a slippery slope, and she hoped with some time to think about it she'd be able to explain her reaction. Half of what was making her crazy was something she wasn't allowed to share, and that was a huge part of the problem.

Maybe it was unfair that she not be able to confide in anyone. But who was safe, and how could she determine that?

Like a sentry riding into the scene on stage bearing news, her phone rang. It was Gibril. She put on her young, confident professional mask and answered it.

"Hi there. Thank you again for the lovely roses." Halley envisioned the lovely scent and velvety texture of the beautiful blooms.

"It was what you deserve. Nothing is too good for you. Would you be up for a quiet dinner somewhere?" Gibril's voice was soft and enchanting. He was a master at this art.

The thought of having something simple and quiet was appealing, but then she'd be under too much scrutiny from his perceptive wiles, and she wanted to keep the promise she'd made to Morgan, even if she hadn't told him so. She also wanted privacy to speak to the former SEAL buddy of his, if and when he called.

Here I am, waiting again.

"I've had a tough day, Gibril. I need a little down time, I'm afraid." That was the honest truth.

"Again? This is not like you."

"I'm afraid I'm not very good company tonight."

"Nonsense. How about I bring over some take-out?"

"You're very sweet. Perhaps this is just a little let-down from the event in Los Angeles catching up with me. And Crystal says we're sold out for the Summit, so I've got to start working on my notes while I'm feeling like I can tackle it. If I wait too long, there will be all those last minute details and emergencies to distract me."

"Exercising good self-care I see. Brava, Halley. I love that about you. You enjoy your flowers, as you work on your life's passion. May they enhance the magic that is your countenance."

"What a lovely thing to say."

"Poetry. I stole that line from an ancient book written over a thousand years ago. I'll bring you a copy sometime."

"Thank you. I'd like that." Halley was very close to caving in to his request when she received notice that another call was coming in. "Gibril, I'm afraid I have to take another call. We'll talk tomorrow, okay?"

"Tomorrow then."

She pressed the hangup/answer button. "This is Halley."

"I'm the friend of Morgan's."

"Oh yes, J.J. He said you'd be calling."

"Well, actually, my name is Hank. Morgan takes to calling me J.J. on occasion. Thanks for picking up."

"No problem."

"Can you walk outside to finish this conversation?"

"Outside?"

"Yes. You have a patio, not too close to another house?"

"This is all getting a little too surreal, J—Hank. I feel like someone is going to pop out of the closet and tell me I've been on a reality television show or something. Very strange for me."

"Just humor me a tiny bit, and I'll get out of your hair."

She walked out the kitchen door into the garage and then onto her backyard patio where a fountain bubbled. "You like the sound of water? Can you hear it?"

"That's very nice. I'm sorry about all this."

"So he told you about our little conversation?"

"Of course. And for the record, I've known Morgan as long, perhaps longer than you have. Everything he told you is one hundred percent true. He and I are working together on this, and, though you and I have never met, I need to get together with you as fast as you can spare the time."

"Are you local?"

"Unfortunately, I'm not." He paused. "Is there any way you could come down south?"

"Where, Coronado?"

"We could meet you in LA if you wanted. I don't want to go into too much detail over the phone, but part of your discussion today revolved around the issue of proof. I can show you this proof. And I think it would be a good idea to do so outside your normal routine. Could you say you have a sick friend you needed to visit?"

"All this clandestine stuff left me bothered all day. I don't do spy very well."

"No, I imagine not. You'll understand after we've had the chance to show you a few things. I'm sure we can answer most of your concerns. Just give us a little of your time, Halley. Please."

"Well, with the event close at hand, it's pure folly to

take a day off, I have so much to do still, but I suppose I could catch a flight to LA tomorrow. I'll see if I can get something tonight to San Diego, if it's easier."

"It would be easier, but either way. We're easy. Just takes us about two-plus hours to drive at night. Your call."

"Can you arrange a motel for me to stay in and pick me up at the airport so I don't have to do any of that?"

"Happy to. You want me to book the flight?"

"Aren't you supposed to be my dying friend? Why would you pay for that? And I just don't know if I can get it together. Let me think about that."

"Gotcha. Okay then, when you have it set up, text your flight itinerary to this number. We'll be there promptly to pick you up, no matter what time. But, Halley, the sooner the better."

"When you say we, you mean Morgan will be there, too?"

"Yes, ma'am."

"Okay then. I'm about to do something so completely out of character, I ought to see a shrink, but I'll be there, and I'll see if I can get a late flight out of SFO tonight. I'm hoping this is all worth it."

"It will be."

CHAPTER 11

J.J. GOT THE text that Halley was able to catch the eight-twenty nonstop direct to San Diego this evening, just as Morgan was pulling up to the house.

"Go take a shower. You stink like hell. Then we'll head over to the airport."

Morgan was glad to get out of the long-sleeved button down shirt he'd nearly tossed out the window on the fast trip up. He felt much better in his cargo pants, Gunny's Gym long-sleeved tee, and his canvas slip-ons. With a leather jacket just in case it turned a little chilly, which wasn't likely, they were good to go.

"You arrange for a place for her for tonight?" he asked as they were leaving.

"Yessir. Nice little one near the Hotel Del, not to far away. Coronado Rose."

"Been there. Good choice."

Outside, J.J. extended his palm. "Your keys."

"My truck, I drive."

"Except you've been driving for over seven hours. My turn," J.J. answered him.

"*Under* seven. No tickets, either." He tossed the keys and climbed in the passenger side of the cab.

"You have gas?"

"Filled up before I left the freeway."

On the way, the two of them said little. They'd decided to do the interview at Morgan's house—the one they owned when they were married, and that left him a little apprehensive. She hadn't been there since. But it was easy and quick and all their stuff was safe there.

The flight was delayed due to fog in San Francisco, which was common, but they hung outside the baggage terminal when they got notice the plane had landed.

Morgan went inside the terminal and found Halley traveling down the hallway toward him. He remembered how she looked those first few times when she visited him before their marriage. He'd felt like the luckiest man in the airport. But this wasn't anything like that. Same airport. Same two people. Totally different feeling and circumstance. He could never have guessed his life would turn out this way.

She had a weekend bag slung over her shoulder, and he didn't ask permission, just lifted it up and put it on his own.

"Thanks for coming tonight," he whispered by way of a greeting. He figured that was the safe way to play it. "J.J. is outside with the truck."

"You mean Hank?"

"Sorry, that's right. You're not the only one getting used to this whole thing."

"I told myself I was being foolish to come down here when I have so much to do. But it was easier to just leave people voicemails and say I was gone. I'll get the questions when I return, but by then, I hope to have some answers for them."

"Good thinking."

"I let my assistant have the day off since I didn't want anyone at the house without me there. I feel like such an inept super sleuth. This whole thing is ridiculous. You know that, don't you?"

"Halley, if I was looking for a way to get you back down here so I could see you again, believe me, I wouldn't make up such a crazy story. You're about to get your eyes opened."

"Yes, around you, my whole world can overturn in a minute. Some things never change."

Her attitude was a bit prickly, but who could blame her? Seeing her ex twice in the same day, surrounded by a plot to blow her and all her followers up wasn't a typical kind of day. Morgan knew her enough still to understand she was masking her insecurity. The banter and slicing little comments made it easier for her to be in his presence. He'd take what he could get. At least she wasn't giving him both barrels between the eyes or her sharp tongue-lashing. His ego was reminding him of how wonderful and artful that tongue could be, in play.

Idiot. You never learn, do you?

He flushed his erotic thoughts and addressed her comment. "At least it's never boring."

Her response was unintelligible.

The truck had just circled again, and J.J. pulled up to the curb. Morgan opened the front door of the cab for Halley, and he climbed in the second seat behind her, placing her carry-on beside him on the bench. She gave a quick glance to be sure.

"I'm Hank," J.J. said as he extended his hand.

"Halley." She didn't extend hers. "So where are we going, or is this top secret, too? Do I wear a blindfold?"

"No, but I can do a body search if you like. No problem, Missy."

"J.J. you said you were married."

"Yes indeed. We're just playing here, Halley, to underscore the rules. Having a bit of fun, right?"

"Oh yea, this is a lot of fun," she said and turned to watch out her passenger window. J.J. made a face in the rear view mirror, and Morgan shrugged in return. It was good he could be casual with her, because Morgan thought it would ease her nerves. He knew by the way she held her head up straight and the angle when she talked she was nervous. He still knew every one of her moves.

She was being as difficult as she could get away with. She'd change her tune once the evidence was laid out in front of her. He was glad J.J. was there to ask some of the questions that would be hot topics for her, especially coming from him. For now, they both just let Halley run her mouth and complain. They were going to make nice until they had to demand cooperation, if it got to that. This wasn't the game she thought it was. He still wasn't one hundred percent sure how she would react to it all once it really sank in.

She was noting some new buildings, changes since she'd been down there. After several minutes, when neither of them commented, she shut up. When they began their troll through Morgan's neighborhood, she turned around to look him straight in the eyes.

"You're not putting me up in your house!"

"No, Halley. We wanna talk first. Then we'll take you to the Coronado Rose. We have your room there. No worries."

She turned back without comment. Sitting behind her, he caught her perfume and saw the long blonde strands of her hair, and he allowed just a tiny piece of his damaged heart to get exposed to a wave of sadness at what had changed. She'd always be the one who got away, even if he was angry as hell with her. She would forever wear that label in his mind. Caution signs were flashing inside him like a freeway accident. On a mission, these were intuitive senses that could keep him safe in an ambush or firefight. He never turned them off, even though, in this case, the mission was entirely different.

J.J. parked the truck in front of the house on Apricot. He'd gotten used to seeing the front yard needed weeding, but today it made him self-conscious. His was the house that made all the others look like perfectly manicured cut outs from a doll set. Some of those ragweeds were nearly three feet tall.

He rolled his shoulder.

It is what it is.

He wasn't here tonight to impress her. He needed to focus on the task at hand. Everything depended on her attitude, because without it, there was that nasty old Plan B.

Morgan grabbed the bag, and Halley let herself out of the truck. She had on one of those bulky sweaters over some tank top underneath with lace that poked dangerously out here and there. But the pants were form-fitting, and it was painful walking behind her.

He slipped ahead, unlocking the front door. That's when he noted it also needed paint.

She stood in the middle of the living room and did a three-sixty, giving the insides a quick rundown.

"You haven't done much to the place."

"I haven't done *anything* to the place," Morgan corrected her. "It's fine, just the way I like it."

She squinted but refrained from making a comment.

J.J. motioned for her to sit at the kitchen table while he got the manila envelope of photographs and write-ups from the Safe Stash in the master bedroom closet. They could make out one of J.J.'s legs in the doorway, indicating he was on his knees retrieving the information.

"Still have your secret box, I see."

"Yup."

"So you never told me how long you've been at this."

They were sitting side by side, and that felt a little too close for comfort. Morgan realized he should offer her something.

"Halley, you want something to drink? A glass of wine? Beer? Or water?"

"I'll take a water," she said to his back as he headed for the refrigerator. He brought her a cold bottle, and one for both he and J.J. as well.

Halley unscrewed the cap and took a huge gulp, returned the cap, and then hesitantly placed it on the table. There was no coaster to protect it from sweating. He reached over and grabbed a napkin from the holder and slid it over to her.

Morgan was getting used to her pointing out all sorts of things he never paid attention to. He didn't know better, but she was trying to keep him off-guard—her form of self-protection. He hoped that disappeared soon. It would be too much to ask for a friendship, but if she trusted him, things would be a whole lot easier.

She got a text that she hid from his view. He'd taken the seat at the end of the table, not chancing to sit next to her again. He tried not to notice as she texted something back. Whoever it was, they were persistent, and there was a bit of back and forth, and then she shut off the notification signal.

Finally, J.J. came in with the big folder. He spread out the paperwork like they'd discussed earlier.

"Halley, these are dossiers on various people who attend a certain mosque in Stockton, California, led by this radical here. Imam." He showed the picture of the handsome cleric.

Halley's head tilted.

"You notice something?" Morgan asked her.

"I've seen this picture before. Fairly sure I've not seen him in person. Has he been in the news?"

"About a year ago. Since then, he's kept a low profile, which is not his real M.O. He likes the spotlight. He likes to be interviewed," J.J. answered. "But look at these photos. We believe one or perhaps many of these people have had ties to him, and may be involved. You recognize anyone here?"

She carefully picked up each and studied them before setting them down. "Sorry. I'm afraid none of these look familiar." She picked up the Imam's photo again. "But this man, I know I've seen a photo with him in it. I was thinking he'd had his eyebrows plucked, you see?"

Morgan had the same reaction. The well-manicured cleric was perfect—too perfect.

"And his skin is so even—almost like he had plastic surgery or something. See how his eyes are evenly pulled back like he had a little tuck?" She motioned with her finger, and Morgan completely saw what she did.

"That's incredible. I'd have never picked up on that," J.J. said with admiration. "What else, Halley?"

"He spends a lot of time on his grooming, don't you think? He doesn't do this himself. He'd have an assistant, that's all I can say." Halley leaned back in her chair and folded her arms. "Maybe that's helpful."

Halley's instincts were spot-on. Neither he nor J.J. had picked up on that. The possibility he'd had plastic surgery to affect some facial recognition software and have more time to fly under the radar would be a smart move for a terrorist.

"I could read all this, but what are you thinking and what are you planning?"

Morgan looked at J.J., who nodded his agreement. "Halley, we need to ask you about your boyfriend, Gibril Messi."

"He's just someone I'm seeing. He knows I'm here."

"He knows you're here? Knows what we're doing here?" Morgan was in a panic.

"No, J.J. and I worked it out that I was visiting a friend dying of cancer. Someone from my past. You don't happen to have cancer, do you, Morgan?"

He wasn't sure she was joking, but he answered anyway. "Very funny. So you told him you were here to visit a friend, then."

"Yes, and that *she* was very ill, so I came down in a hurry to be at her side. I've just deflected all the questions about where I'm staying and which hospital, etc."

J.J. leaned forward. "But you didn't tell him who you were meeting, right? And does he know you're in San Diego?"

"No, as a matter of fact, I told him Los Angeles. I figured that would be safer."

Morgan let out a sigh of relief.

"Halley, is there any reason you might suspect him of any involvement in this? Think hard before you answer." Morgan was glad J.J. had asked that question, but it didn't stop Halley from drilling him a nasty look.

"I don't need time to think about it. He's a wonderful man. I like him for his culture, his success in business, and the way he takes time to enjoy these things. He's a gentleman. I like the respect and the way he treats me. Any woman would."

Morgan didn't want to see her face as she delivered this line. He was guilty on all counts. But he was in for the short or long of it. No matter how much it hurt, if it would help get her cooperation and keep her safe, help find these cretins, he'd put up with the dredging up of his mistakes from the past. And yes, he deserved punishment for them all.

"But you haven't told me if you think he's involved," J.J. persisted.

"You mean is he being nice to me just to con me into thinking he really cares? Like so he can jump on my bones? I'm experienced with that."

Morgan didn't think she was thinking of him. Perhaps she'd had more of a rough patch than he'd realized during their years apart. He couldn't hold back any longer. "No, Halley, so he can kill you and all the women who attend your seminars." He didn't smile. He wasn't afraid of how it would make her feel. She had to get the reason they were all getting together.

Halley swallowed, then grabbed her bottle, and drank. Morgan noticed her hand was shaking.

"That's a good sign, Halley," Morgan said as he pointed to her hand. "You should be scared. You should be damned scared. You may not like it, but someone near or close to you is probably in on this plot. You cannot trust anyone."

"Anyone?" she said too quickly.

"Don't play games, Halley." He decided to let her have it the same way she'd done to him. "Don't flatter yourself to think that there's any other reason I'm here talking to you than because of this terrorist thing. I don't want to be here any more than you want your life turned upside-down. But we got to work together. Otherwise, you—well, all three of us are in danger." He saw J.J. nodding furiously.

Halley was breathing heavily, and, thank God, she apologized with her eyes closed.

"I'm sorry. It's only been a few hours since all this was thrown in my face. I'm trying to keep up, as usual."

"That's okay," J.J. said, patting her hand. "We thank you for trying your very best. All we can ask. It's a big help having you here so quickly."

"We should have sent J.J. there in the first place," Morgan grumbled and crossed his arms and legs.

"Cut it out. Quit feeling sorry for yourself, Hansen," J.J. barked.

"So can I just ask you guys how you got the tip that lead to this investigation? I mean, nasty people are all around the U.S. I'm sure this guy was on the FBI's radar for a long time before now. So, of all the jerks out there who might want to do something, why do you think they targeted me?"

"You spoke to a Muslim girls' school near Sacramento last year, right?" asked J.J.

"I did. They loved it. Invited me back. Several of those girls will be at my Hero Summit in Hawaii next summer."

"The FBI forwarded this article in the local mosque newsletter. This wasn't a general circulation publication. Only reserved for senior staff and revered worshipers."

Morgan followed up by placing the photocopy right in front of her. At the top of the article was a picture of Halley, with a bull's eye centered over her torso.

"I have the translation of this if you want to read it. But it gives information about your events, including a link to your website where all your travel dates are listed, along with where you're speaking. We think this was the seed of what later became an operation," he continued.

"I just remembered. Got a cryptic response to my last blog post—something about leading women down the path to destruction."

"That's pretty irrefutable evidence. Can we get our

guys to look at it?"

"I deleted it."

"Then we'll need your computer," said J.J.

"Hold on a minute. I have all my life stored on this computer." She pointed to her briefcase. "I never go anywhere without it."

J.J. and Morgan exchanged a glance.

"Halley, we've got lots of trails we're trying to follow, but I think we need to get one of our guys over here to check your computer out. If someone wanted to track your whereabouts, they could do it through your laptop," Morgan said softly.

"But my work—"

He chose to interrupt her by gently placing his hand over hers on the table. "Halley, we'll protect your work. I think it's time to buy yourself another computer. We can download everything you feel is critically important, protect everything else. But we have to get our specialists on it to at least find out if there are any strings we can pull or other paths to follow. It's a start."

She was watching his hand covering hers. Very slowly, she slid her palm back, placing it on her lap beneath the table, and took a deep breath.

"He's right, Halley. We have to turn this thing in. It might be infected with all kinds of malware and tracking devices. And if not, well, at least we'll know."

"If they're tracking me, they know I'm here, at this

address."

"Have you opened your laptop since you landed?" J.J. asked.

"No, not yet."

"Then you buy a new one while we get this one looked at. I'll take you tomorrow to get that accomplished," Morgan added.

"I just feel like all my clothes have been ripped off me. Everything of my personal life is on that computer. Everything I've been working on for several years. My book, my seminars, the content for the event in San Jose. All my personal emails and conversations with vendors, helpers, and fans. How will I replace all that?"

"Eventually. But isn't it worth it if it will keep you safe?" J.J. asked.

Morgan thought he knew what would really strike home for Halley. "If we can get a jump on things, perhaps we won't have to cancel the event. Without your computer, our hands are tied."

Her answer was to pull her red laptop out of her briefcase and hand it to J.J. She didn't hand it to Morgan, but that was okay. She was on board, and at least they were starting to get somewhere.

J.J. gave her a thumbs-up. "Good girl."

CHAPTER 12

MORGAN TOOK HALLEY to the Coronado Rose, followed her up to her room, checked all the windows, and double-checked the locking device on the door. He peeled off two hundred dollar bills and handed them to her.

"We've got you under the name Jenny Horn, just so you know. We've booked tomorrow night, too, just in case, so housekeeping won't bug you about a move time in the morning. I'll try to call the room in the morning and touch base, okay?"

"Fine."

"Use cash for room service. Don't sign anything or give your name to anyone, but if you're calling the front desk, you're Jenny, okay?"

"Or, I thought that was payment in advance for services." She gave him a royal smirk.

"Very funny. I'm serious about all this, Halley. You've got to remember not to use your real name anywhere or be seen."

"I think I can manage to follow that without screwing up, I think."

She looked at the money again. It made her feel awkward, but she planned to take a long hot shower and just crash. She'd see how the information settled after a good night's sleep and a morning meditation.

"So I can't use my cell? You know I used it to text Gibril?"

"Don't answer anybody's calls or texts on that phone, and don't open it up until I get an okay. We'll get you a phone you can use tomorrow. Just hold off everything until we do some checking. I'm thinking you could let people know you got your computer ripped off in the airport, something like that? We might have to do that with the cell as well."

"So you're thinking I have to turn that in, also?"

"Waiting to find out. So please don't use it to tip anyone off."

"Don't they have tracking devices on them?" she asked. Here she was asking for advice from the one man she thought she'd never trust again. But she saw how hard he was trying.

"Halley, I never had to deal with this shit, so I have no idea." He did look like a kid again. And she liked that he was being honest.

She pulled the phone out and handed it to him. "Then you take it. No peeking. I don't give you permission to go digging into places you don't belong."

"Got your message loud and clear. No worries there. I wouldn't want to mess up the big boys. Wouldn't be very smart, would it?"

She caught him checking out her sweater. No doubt standing with her, alone in a motel room, brought back memories of their early days when none of this was on the horizon. When he realized he'd been caught, that quick red face gave him away.

"Sorry."

It was the way he was wired up. For all of Gibril's refinement, Morgan had power and forward momentum. He was a rocket shot out of a cannon, and Gibril was like a walk in a beautiful forest. They couldn't be more opposite.

She decided to send him an olive branch, not to encourage him, but just to put water on some of the fires that had been burning for both of them for ten years.

"Like I said to you at the house, I know this is difficult for you, too. Thank you for trying. And thank you for caring about my welfare, even if it is a job and a paycheck."

She was hoping he'd take the joke, and she could see it stung a bit, but he softened. "It's much more than a job and a paycheck. I mean that from the bottom of my heart."

They stared into each other's eyes for several seconds. They never used to do this. It was all go at it, get to the sex or the argument. But tonight, they just looked at each other's faces and absorbed what they saw. She saw a man damaged by his own hand and burdened by a past that wasn't his fault. She saw a man who had one speed, and that was fast. On. Present. No daydreams or visions of greatness. He used to tell her he was just a man who was hired "to get 'er done" because he could. He did the things others couldn't do, and for that, he'd paid a heavy price. But he also didn't want anyone's pity.

And she was a woman who couldn't take the energy because it interfered with her own. He needed someone who could support him. She needed the same thing, and neither one could give the other what was needed. That was the long and the short of it.

Unmasked and without the emotional overtones, the angry upsets, and hurts, she could see better who this man really was. And he wasn't so threatening. Or maybe he'd learned to couch some things, change his behavior in ways she'd not noticed. This could be the way he was all along, and she just never saw it.

Any way she served it up, she came to the same conclusion. She'd heard people say it on military blogs or at functions she used to attend. She'd seen it written on a plaque located on an island in the South Pacific, carved by men who knew what they were talking about and who'd just lost their best friends on a foreign beach. She stepped toward him without touching, inhaled, and said, "Thank you, Morgan for all you've done and continue to do to keep me safe. Thank you for my freedom. I appreciate you more than I've ever told you before."

He was going to grab her and kiss her, but she pushed him away.

"Whoa! I didn't mean *that*. I said 'thank you', not 'come fuck me.'"

His smirk was so disarming, in spite of how wrong it was to love seeing it. He was forbidden fruit all the way. Every part of him. The way he looked, the imaginary way he made love to her in her dreams—full tilt without holding anything back. He made quick decisions just like she did, like it was ready, fire, and then aim. He'd always give his all and bear the consequences of the haunting afterward. He wouldn't change for anyone or anything because being damaged looked good on him. Like a uniform that was perfectly tailored. His scars were his medals. He was a hurricane sometimes without a focus, and he'd never be tethered to anyone, no matter what the cost. But he could, and she honestly believed this with her whole heart, that he could save her from whomever was after her.

Just before he opened the door, he turned. "Darlin', I'm revved and ready to go if and when you ever decide to drop that gate."

CHAPTER 13

J.J. HAD GOTTEN permission for the new disconnected SEALs from Kyle's squad to come for an interview, so they scheduled it for ten. They were to use the Federal Building downtown, which Commander Lambert had set up. Lambert also got J.J.'s apartment cleared and a five thousand dollar stipend for Morgan. Both men would have the keys delivered to their box later in the afternoon, along with the address.

Morgan was told Lambert was pleased with Halley's cooperation, anxious to get eyes on her computer and laptop. They were to leave them with Lambert's associate in San Diego so they could be sent back to Quantico.

Morgan took a chance and dialed Halley's room from J.J.'s burner. He wasn't sure if she'd pick up.

"How you holding up?"

"I didn't sleep well, even with the hot shower. I've

had breakfast. When do I get my computer? And I'll need a phone. Are you guys going to take me?"

"We have an interview in about an hour. Can you hold off until after then, say closer to noon? Remember, do not go outside the room for any reason. Room service is okay."

"Okay. How did *you* sleep?"

"I slept better after the sixth cold shower." He exaggerated it a bit. He'd only taken three.

She giggled, and it was the first time in ten years he'd heard that.

Damn!

There was nothing worse than having a stiffy and not having a way to cure it. He had little hope Halley had decided to be that cozy, but things were definitely heading in that direction. He was also a realist and knew under pressure people did things they wouldn't do otherwise. Her fear could be making her more needy, and he had to be ready for that. He was going to play it completely hands-off.

When they arrived at the interview room, the two young former SEALs had already arrived and been given coffee. They looked like high school kids caught for stealing a government car. Their bright orange hair looked like it came out of a bottle. No way they would pass for any Middle Eastern terrorist.

"I'm Stanley," the taller one said as he extended his

long arm for a shake.

"And I'm Taylor," the shorter one said with a slight Southern accent.

Morgan and J.J. introduced themselves, as well. J.J. motioned for them to sit down. "So what did Kyle tell you about this operation?"

Stanley volunteered first. "Well, first of all, he said you might have a place for us. Wouldn't be exactly the Navy, but you might be able to use our assets."

"And you needed someone who could interpret, perhaps more?" added Taylor.

"Did he say where this mission might be?" Morgan asked.

"Well, it's kind of not a secret somebody high level is recruiting SEALs. We were kinda hoping that was the gig. But we're looking for any good opportunity to get blown up or shot at," Taylor answered.

The two friends chuckled at their own joke. Morgan didn't think it was funny. It was obvious they'd not been overseas yet, where the Gates of Hell were located. Seeing them changed a man, and they didn't give off that vibe.

J.J. spread out a couple of pictures and then handed them the article in Arabic with Halley's picture at the top. "You recognize any of these actors?"

The boys shook their heads. Stanley squinted at the newsletter post. "You want me to read this to you? We both can read and write Arabic. We know a lot of the dialects, too."

"Knock yourself out," Morgan instructed.

In unison, they read the short article. Their voice inflections were nearly perfect. With his eyes closed, Morgan could feel like he was listening to a native speaker. Both he and J.J. were impressed. Kyle was right.

"Impressive, although I wouldn't know if you were just reading me gibberish, but kudos. You've studied well, gents."

J.J. nodded agreement.

"Yessir. We take to languages like riding a bike," said Taylor.

"Wish we'd had you on some of the missions we did in the sand box," Morgan answered. "Could have used you. We could never find enough interpreters especially ones we could trust."

"That was our plan, but..." Stanley shrugged.

"Okay, so here we have it in a nutshell, and I have to know today if you're in or out," J.J. began. "We have a likely threat against this woman,"—he put his fore-finger on Halley's picture—"but we believe they will be making an example of her at a very public forum. She has a large workshop coming up in San Jose in about three weeks. We need to stop the people from carrying out this attack."

"That's cool," said Stanley.

"Who would we be working for?" asked Taylor.

"We're under a covert division of the CIA, run by retired Commander Greg Lambert. They're the brains; we're the grunts in the field. We need you guys to infiltrate this mosque." He showed them the pictures of the Imam in front of his house of prayer. "Someone here knows about what's going to happen. If you can, we need you to quickly get inside or learn who is inside and how they plan on doing the deed."

Both boys were enthusiastic.

"If you have a needle, we'll sign in blood, sir," said Taylor.

Morgan chuckled. He remembered being so gung-ho. "You do know this is a temporary assignment. No guarantee there will be another. But I've been authorized to tell you the CIA is watching you very closely, and if this works out, you might have a new job working permanently for them. This one is purely undercover. You'll have to completely disassociate yourselves from your family and most of your friends."

"I got no family, sir," Stanley said as if he was proud of it. "But Taylor here has eleven sisters."

Morgan laughed. "Tell me they don't live in San Diego, please!"

"Nosir. They're all in North Carolina with my folks. They don't get out here much at all, and I never can go home. They parade their friends in front of me. Those girls won't leave me alone. Nosir, I never go home."

"I thought I detected that Palmetto accent," said J.J.

"So you guys will have to figure out some story to get inside. I assume you know the customs, right? You can pass for a real Muslim?" Morgan asked.

"Sure can do. But I think we want to look like we don't know it all," said Taylor. "Like we're lost. We just got booted from the Teams, and we're disillusioned."

"Some men in your situation would be," said J.J.

"You'll have to figure out a way you came to the faith and all," added Morgan.

"I think we could say we studied the language, as part of our training. And then, somehow, we got the real story of why U.S. troops were there, and we felt we wanted to support the freedom cause, something like that." Taylor looked at Stanley, who nodded. "We'll work on it."

"Sounds good to me," said J.J. "I can't let you have these things here, so commit them to memory. You'll need to buy a couple of burner phones and give me the numbers, and from now on, only use those phones. Store you cells for after the mission, okay? Tell your families you're traveling, broadening your education so they don't go to the police or bug the Navy, okay?"

"Sure thing. I can do that," said Taylor.

"I got this paperwork you have to fill out and turn

in here. They're going to take your picture for internal I.D. But you understand, if you get caught, no one knows about you and there won't be anyone coming to your aid. Unlike the SEAL teams, there's no backup. But Morgan and I here will go overboard to make sure you make it out alive. No guarantees."

"I like it. Just what I signed up for when I originally got my Trident."

"They let you keep it?" Morgan wanted to know.

"Until they ask for it back. But no one's gonna see it," Taylor whispered and then followed up with a grin.

After the boys were fingerprinted and photographed and signed the application form for "Special Duty Officer-Counter Terrorism Expert," Morgan congratulated them. They were given J.J.'s contact information, along with five hundred dollars each, and asked to check in tomorrow morning. They'd be staying in an apartment the CIA would be arranging for them near the Mosque in Stockton.

"Wait! We have to live in Stockton?" asked Stanley.

J.J. and Morgan froze.

"Just kidding. That's up by the San Francisco Bay, right?"

"Yes, on the east side of the bay," answered Morgan. "Better than Beauford, North Carolina." He grinned at Taylor.

"Don't knock it," Taylor quipped back. "I always

say, Beauford population: One hundred thirty-two. Number of teeth per population: Sixty."

"I'm sure the founding fathers are delighted with your description," chuckled J.J. "But I happen to know it's pretty country. All of it is pretty."

"Welcome to the team," said Morgan.

"Thank you, sir."

Morgan checked his watch. He had a half-hour before he needed to pick up Halley. "I got to get you back to your truck. Supposed to pick up Halley at noon at the Rose."

"We're done here."

On the way back to Apricot street, J.J. flew a couple of questions his way. "Looks like you and Halley are getting along better. Anything happen I need to know about last night when you took her home?"

"Not a thing," Morgan answered.

"And I notice she hasn't requested I take her to buy the new computer."

Morgan just shrugged and kept driving. "I'd not read anything too much into it. She's scared. Just clinging to the familiar, perhaps. Doesn't mean she's surrendered her body or anything."

J.J. sighed. "Miracles can happen, my friend."

"Yea, but not to me."

MORGAN WAS ON time. He walked casually into the

lobby, wearing another button-down shirt he usually hated. And this one was pink, on top of it all, but he knew Halley would love it.

He even polished a pair of brown loafers and wore socks that matched his trousers. But he left his stubble from yesterday and applied a tad of J.J.'s aftershave. He knocked. Halley was glowing in another sweater, this time red. She could wear red better than anyone else he knew. With the red lipstick, she could have been the real life Jessica Rabbit with her small waist and over-sized but well-formed chest. She had on a skirt with red heels to match her sweater. It was borderline siren package territory. She was being a tease on purpose.

"You look terrific in pink, Morgan. Never seen you wear that before."

Bingo.

"And you know full well what you're doing to me, Halley." He leaned against the doorframe, crossing his ankles because his dick had gotten to be the size of a gorilla's.

"Well, it's not my problem," she said, batting her eyes, and then giving him one luscious smile.

The fact that he knew what she tasted like, how she quivered when he rubbed her little nub with his tongue or made her breasts jiggle, that he'd explored more of her than everyone else combined, and still couldn't get enough made it ten times worse. He was always sorry when he came, wishing the joining and the coming together could last for a whole hour, perhaps whole day. It was that special. He let her see it in his eyes, if she dared.

She stopped the ridiculous exaggeration of her eye fluffing, lowered her chin, and just stared back to him. He could see the vein at the right side of her neck pulsing and, unless he was crazy, could smell her arousal.

But he was strictly hands-off. She'd have to strip him naked if she wanted anything from him sexually. And for that possible pleasure, he'd let her lead him all over the shopping mall by his dick if it needed to happen that way. He'd be walking knock-kneed and buck-footed to protect the package that felt like it sunk all the way to below his mid-thigh. He was a throbbing jumble of veins and constrained muscle tissue trying to break free. He'd pay for this dearly.

It's all worth it.

"You're not coming in?" she asked.

He dipped his head inside and scanned the room. Her bed was unmade, and a light pink nightie was slung over the wing chair in the corner. "I don't see any computers here. I think we'd have better luck at the Apple store, don't you?"

She picked up her purse, inserted her room key into the little zipper pocket in front, and slipped by him.

He didn't move and accepted whatever she wanted to give him, but he wouldn't grab her. Her thigh got an idea how hard he was, and she hesitated there and then continued to the hallway and toward the elevators without looking back.

Morgan sucked in air and closed the door, ambling down behind her, and then running because the elevator doors had opened.

There was an older couple inside, dressed in tennis garb. They appeared to be in their seventies and in better shape than some of the SEAL wives in their twenties. Nobody said a word. Halley didn't have to. Her perfume did all the talking, as did the rising and lowering of her chest.

He stumbled on the slight difference in surface at the elevator opening but righted himself before he'd have to brace on anything. His hands felt awkward and his feet clumsy. He chalked it up to the shoes he was unfamiliar wearing.

At the shopping mall, they found the Apple Store and were able to get a salesman to help them without making an appointment. He let her do all the talking, since he didn't even own a laptop.

They didn't have any red laptop covers, so she bought hers in white instead of silver. She was going to pay for it and then remembered the rule about using her credit cards. "I didn't think about this," she said in astonishment.

"I did." Morgan had gotten four thousand dollars from J.J.s credit card, and he handed over the wad of bills for the sale.

"Purchase contract?" The young, cheerful salesman wanted them to buy an extended warranty.

"Not yet. I'll think about it."

"The lady also needs to register this under a new gmail account. Can you show her how to set that up?" Morgan asked.

"Certainly! We don't cover Google or Google products, but I have gmail and can show her how to set up a new one."

Within minutes, she was set up, and the purchase was completed.

She was given instructions and partially shown how to retrieve things from the cloud so she could access some of her old computer files. She was pleased when her program notes and the rough draft start of her next book were also stored properly. Morgan would have to say she was almost giddy with delight. He loved being around that side of her.

With the computer purchased, he carried the large box out to the truck and met her at the phone store, where Halley picked out a beautiful phone, but it wasn't a burner.

"No, this isn't going to work." He leaned into the

counter and asked the young attendant what he wanted.

"Okay, gotcha. I didn't pick up on that. When she said prepaid—"

"No worries. And son, make that two. I need one, too."

It took less than ten minutes to get their new phones. First call he made as they were walking out to the parking lot was to J.J.

"I'm hooked up. Halley has her computer and her phone." She showed him the number written on the outside of the box. "We requested a 650 area code for Halley." He gave J.J. both numbers.

"Good going. I got our apartment and the keys. Going over later to take a look and show the boys. You wanna tag along?"

"Let me see how it goes with Halley. See if she needs anything." He glanced her way, but she pretended not to notice. "I think she'll want to fly home tomorrow, so is there anything we need from her first?"

That got Halley's attention. She didn't object, so Morgan had figured right about her timing.

"We should try to get in one more meeting. They should have the computer and the phone tomorrow morning, and I'll call Lambert to see if they have questions before she leaves. But at least now she can call her assistant, and we need to talk about the boy-friend. Put your thinking cap on."

"Will do. Will check in when I'm returning back to my house."

"I'm not going to take the guys over there. So to-morrow's meeting will be at the apartment. We'll talk in the morning."

"Gotcha."

"Hey, Morgan?"

"Yea?"

"Behave yourself."

"Always. No worries there. I have it all figured out."

"I'll just bet you do."

CHAPTER 14

H ALLEY SAID LITTLE on their short trip back to the Coronado Rose. She had checked for a return flight and booked the five-thirty. That gave them more time to discuss strategy and get their instructions straight. She was glad there would be one more meeting, since she didn't want to pack everything into tonight and then battle the crowds getting home. Being out of her element, her normal daily routine seemed to be good for her. But she knew it wasn't something that would last.

Morgan was patient while she texted Gibril and let him know she'd be returning tomorrow evening. She tried calling Crystal but got no answer, so she left a message to take one more day off, and she'd see her on Wednesday. She arranged for a driver to meet her at the airport for the ride home. She tried to check her phone's voicemail, but she couldn't access it. Her landline at the house was barely used, and since she'd long ago forgotten her password, she couldn't access that voicemail, either.

In short, her real life was going to have to wait another day. She'd pick up the pieces, hoping that tomorrow's meeting would give her some direction. If it was possible to still do the event, she would. If it was safest not to, well, then she'd have to cancel. She understood it did no good to stand up and show she was unafraid if it got everybody killed.

Morgan parked the truck and came around quickly to help her from the cab. He carried the large box for her laptop, while Halley brought the bag with some accessories and the two cell phone boxes. They waded through the lobby and took the first elevator available, which was nearly packed with people. Morgan was able to squeeze in, and he pulled Halley in with him. One by one, the cage began to thin out until they were alone at the top floor, where her room was.

She unlocked her door and laid the packages on the bed. Morgan opened up her computer box and took out the laptop, the cord, and all the components and manuals, neatly packaged in the signature white boxes. He plugged it in to charge but didn't open it.

"It will take me days to update all my passcodes, reauthorize my online banking, and reset my social media."

"Maybe you don't need as many as you thought.

Maybe lightening up would be a good thing, not a bad thing."

"But I need—" She stopped herself as she began to see Morgan's eyes glass over. "Funny how we just keep adding things until we don't know what we're doing it for, and all of a sudden we have this massive machine we have to try to control. It would be like me trying to operate a Harley."

"I understand your need to be out there in the news, using social media to promote your seminars. But now you understand there are risks."

"Nothing is totally risk-free," she said and then quickly regretted it.

Morgan had been standing with his back to her, outlining the edges of her computer with his forefinger. He made a half-turn and stood in profile, admiring the view from her window. The sunset was just about to start, and the glow looked otherworldly.

When she joined him, she felt the dying sun's heat reflected off the window glass. He didn't touch her, and she could tell he wanted to.

"Are you hungry?" she asked.

"Not exactly," he said to the window. He still wasn't making eye contact, but his left hand was fisting and unfisting. She knew something was brewing inside him.

"Can you stay?" She wasn't sure it was her own

voice calling to him. He slowly peeled his eyes off the orange horizon.

"You want me to stay?"

"Is it allowed under your mission rules?"

He adjusted so he was directly facing her now. "I was ordered to behave. I gave my word."

She was watching the side of his face pick up the orange from the sunset and followed the shape of his moist lips after he licked them. His huge shoulders loomed larger than she'd ever remembered before. He wore a spicy cologne that was delicate and not at all fitting the man in front of her, as if it belonged to a school boy. Morgan was so many pieces, and her body went so many places just watching him. It was clear he would not make a move to touch her, so she had to touch him.

She stepped closer, felt the heat of his body barely touching hers, as she placed one palm over his heart. He quickly responded by pressing it hard against him.

"It's been a long time, Morgan," she whispered as his face came closer, as his mouth opened just before she closed her eyes.

"Too long," he whispered to her lips as he first brushed against them and then inhaled and kissed her deeply.

Her pulse soared as her knees wobbled. He braced her shaking body with his arm at her back, fingers splayed at her shoulder blades, holding and pressing her into his chest.

She couldn't believe what was happening. He was ready to devour her, his probing fingers halfway up her thigh, sliding her skirt up and hooking her panties. She was wet as the tips of his fingers found her core. When his thumb pressed against her nub, she nearly fainted.

"Tell me, Halley, what you want," he whispered to her ear. His fingers were rubbing the back of her skull, having their way with her hair. He was kissing her temple, running a tongue around the arch in her ear, ending with a nip to her earlobe impaled with a single stud diamond.

"I—I'm having trouble thinking," she sighed into him.

"Tell me what you're thinking, and I'll help."

He had slid his palm up and under her sweater, delicately rolling it up and over her head and then dropping it to the floor. He took a step back to look at her, his lips still wet from their kisses. "Tell me," he repeated. "I want to know what you want."

She was desperate for his touch. "I'm thinking about all the times I've wondered what it would be like to pretend that the last ten years never happened. Can you make those go away, Morgan?"

He began unbuttoning his shirt, all the time watching her remove her bra. He finished with the cuffs and then let the thing fall to the ground near her sweater. She put her thumbs under the hem of his tee shirt and slowly pulled it up over his beautiful, hard body. His muscles rippled as he cupped her elbows with his palms and slowly drew her forward to him. He watched her knotted nipples touch his flesh. His huge hands lifted her butt cheeks and pressed her hard against his erection with such strength that her feet were nearly airborne.

He raised his knee slightly into position, and she rode his thigh, lazily rubbing the lips of her sex against him, hands gripping the back of his neck to pull herself up and then down hard against him. The delicious pulsing of her sweet spot began to set her insides on fire, just as his teeth and tongue found her left nipple. She touched his cheek, laced the back of her hand against the stubble, and then lined his lips with her forefinger before he sucked it.

"What is it you want from me, Halley?"

She climbed higher, pulling herself up so she could whisper in his ear. "I want you to fuck me, Morgan."

"Yes, ma'am. That's what I'm going to do alright. But, honey, just after you get those lips on my cock. I'm about to explode."

She shimmied his pants down over his hips, smoothing his backside with her palms while she dropped to her knees. He was working the zipper on her skirt, leaning over while she rooted for him. Just as she took him into her mouth, rolling her tongue over the heavy veins and trying to accommodate his huge size, he had lowered her skirt down to her knees and was tracing the deep cleft in her rear.

She could feel Morgan tense, so she stopped her sucking and just rolled her tongue over his tip, released him, and then took him back deep again. At his groan, she thought he was going to spill so she stopped again, allowing him to pull out and feel the tension of her suck.

"Geez, Halley! I gotta get inside you, but man, I don't want you to stop."

She massaged his balls and worked his shaft with both hands. "You want me to stop? I can hardly take you in my mouth already." She kissed his tip and got to her feet. Her skirt dropped to the floor so that she was standing naked in front of him, wearing her red high heels.

Morgan stepped out of his pants around his ankles and abruptly picked her up and threw her on the bed. She spread her knees and arched her back, digging the red heels into the bed covers, calling to him with her arms.

He dove in, throwing one leg over his shoulder, laving her lips with the stiff curl of his tongue, sucking her bud, and making her jump. He brought his thumb to press that little organ, inserted two fingers inside her, and watched the pleasure she took. Her body was on fire, and an orgasm had started to stretch across her insides, flushing her core with juices.

He quickly grabbed one of the pillows and pushed it beneath the small of her back, raising her pelvis to him while he got to his knees, rocked over her shattering body, and plugged her deep. The force of his entry nearly took her breath away as he then gradually began a rhythm of strokes, each one deeper than the next. She was hanging onto him then wrapping her legs around his waist as she worked in unison with his heavy thrusts. Her red heels were lightly tapping against his buttocks.

He switched angles and pumped her from the side. Halley clutched the pillow to her chest, feeling her internal muscles milking him, the orgasm taking full hold of her body now.

Just when she thought she couldn't take any more, he flipped her to her stomach, stuffed the pillow beneath her belly, and slowly entered her from behind, letting her feel every inch of him. She rocked back on him, arching her back, her knees on the outsides of his as she straddled his groin backwards, causing him to split her open and go deeper still. His hands squeezed her breasts almost to the point of pain. His fingers sparked her swollen and overworked bud. She went over the edge, holding herself down on him as deep as he could go. The answering pulsation deep within her core confirmed he was filling her with everything he had.

He kissed her until her body stopped shaking. Clutching her now-wet body to his upper torso, he lifted them, still joined by his shaft, and drew the covers up over them both.

"Morgan, I missed you."

"I'm right here, Halley. Not going anywhere." He thrust against her insides again to underscore the point. "I'm gonna ride with you all night long, honey. I haven't even begun to show you how I've missed this."

She was falling into a warm, dreamlike sleep, her body feeding off the energy he was sending out. "All night?" she asked.

"Sleep's overrated. You don't need sleep, honey; you need this."

His back and forth movements returned. Within minutes, she had become a rag doll. Her hair was soaking, and the sheets were damp with their combined sweat. But he wouldn't leave her alone. He stayed deep inside until she could no longer keep her eyes open. Even then, she had just the energy to say, "Don't stop."

"I'm here for as long as you can put up with me, sweetheart."

She clung to his chest, finding his warm torso the pillow she'd sleep on and dream about. What had been impossible had suddenly turned possible.

CHAPTER 15

MORGAN WATCHED THE streaks of early pre-dawn turn her hair into ringlets of spun gold. The gentle perfume between her breasts had lingered with him for most the night, bringing back all the old memories—the good ones. He remembered the first time they'd made love, discovering she was as intense as he was. Waiting became an impossibility when they were first together. Everything about the world sent them back to the bedroom or the living room couch, even in a bookstore or coffee shop if he took her dare, which he often did.

She slept as hard as she made love. Her breath strong, her legs still possessively wrapped around his waist so his cock could remain buried in her warmth.

He lifted a few strands from her forehead and eyes and kissed them one at a time. "Wake up, sleepyhead."

"I can't move."

"Yes, you can, because I have to go pee."

"Then take me with you." She began to giggle, just like she used to.

He picked her up and carried her into the bathroom. "No, wait, Morgan. I didn't mean it."

He opened the shower door and deposited her there, reaching to turn on the water. She gave him a sultry smile and began rubbing her breasts again, rocking her hips from side to side. He was trying to pee, and it wasn't working. He'd slept the last two hours with an incredibly full bladder.

He had to turn away or he'd not be able to go, and that worked. He joined her under the warm spray.

"How do you feel?" he asked her.

"Used."

"Used? That's not a good thing."

She was wobbly again, her eyes closed as she let the warm water pour over the top of her head while she washed with soap. Next came the giggle, that little drunken stupor of sex, and finally the words. "Morgan, it's a very good thing. You know it is. I can hardly move. I love it."

"Really?" he said as he turned her body around, pressing her backside into his groin.

He pulled his knees under hers so that she could sit back on him. His shaft entered her swollen lips from behind, and she hugged herself and moaned a gentle, "Ow."

"Am I hurting you?"

She giggled again. "Um hum," she whispered, kissing the sides of the tile wall. "I like it, baby. My fault entirely for being out of practice."

"Nonsense. Nothing's changed. It's only gotten better, Halley."

He held her while she groaned into the wall as he thrust upward and drove home to oblivion.

Afterward, they returned to the bed, and she slept with her backside to him in the rose-colored terry robe the hotel provided, the tie opened so he could stroke her smooth skin while she slept. He seemed not to be able to get enough of the touch of her silky flesh. He wondered how all this would change any of the scenarios. He'd willingly put all that out of his mind, but now, he recalled J.J.'s words of last night, *'We have to deal with the boyfriend.'*

What exactly did that mean? Was he now going to take the place the handsome Gibril had occupied previously? Or could she play with them both, and what would he do about it if that was her choice? He hadn't asked her that. It wasn't a condition of their mating last night. He was so starved for the feel of her body against and around his that he deemed unimportant what the meaning was.

In the light of day, with the memory of their night of passion still playing re-runs throughout his head, he knew some of these things would get resolved or this night would be tucked away into the memory box and stored until they were ready to look at it again. Because his primary purpose was to keep her safe by foiling the plot, not to keep her happy and fed in bed all day. Her safety was far more important than his drive to possess her.

Perhaps Gibril will come after me. Would that help?

Of course, this assumed he was the accomplice of the Imam, which still hadn't been established. Morgan decided he'd visit him in his office, use a ruse to meet with him. See if the gentleman could show Morgan his guilty side when he didn't think anyone was looking.

He wondered if Halley would still have feelings for the Middle Eastern man. Or would he be able to tell there had been a shift in her behavior? Would this compromise the mission? He hoped not.

At nine, they were awakened by the housekeeping staff. Checkout was at eleven, they said. It was a shocking reminder that the wonderful evening they spent together was now at an end. They were dressed within minutes. As Halley blow-dried her hair, he saw her gather herself together, just like he was, preparing for business.

Morgan ordered breakfast and texted J.J. they'd be ready in about an hour.

Call me when you're leaving, you prick. J.J. followed it

with another text giving him the address to the apartment.

The room service tray arrived, and he paid for it in cash, leaving a generous tip for the server.

"You're still wearing the pink shirt. I love that shirt on you," she said over the top of her coffee cup.

He shrugged. "Well, I didn't expect this. You've got me in pink for a second day then."

"Should we get the CIA to spring for another shirt?"

"I'm good. Besides we have no time. But thanks." He thought about the questions he wanted to ask her. Before he could open his mouth, Halley's phone buzzed, and she picked it up. He knew who it was immediately by her conflicted expression.

"I'm fine. Coming home this evening. Just a little tired with all the drama." She glanced up at Morgan, who stopped a forkful of eggs in midair. He mouthed *drama* and scrunched up his face in a question mark.

Halley continued with the conversation after giving Morgan a pert smile. "We've said our good-byes, but I'll go see her one more time this morning. Her family is with her now from the East Coast, so my work is done." After she listened further, she answered again. "A friend of mine from modeling days. Very old friend." Then she answered another question. "She's in a hospice care facility." She gave another sweet smile to

Morgan and then sipped her coffee. "Well, that's because my computer was stolen at the airport. Just got a new one yesterday, and I've got a new gmail account. Everything isn't set up yet. I'll try to work on it tonight. But at least you have my cell. Listen, no more questions, okay? We can talk tomorrow perhaps."

Morgan watched her sign off. "Yes, I'll text you when I'm home," and then, "No, I already have the driver set up, but thanks. I'm really exhausted, Gibril. I need sleep."

Her sweet blush was a thing of beauty.

She set the phone down with a big sigh. "How did I do?"

"I loved the blush at the end especially."

She blushed again and took a sip of orange juice.

"He sure asks a lot of questions. You don't find that suspicious?

"I guess I'm used to it, but it did make me a little nervous. I think he might know something's up."

"Are you really exhausted? Because I feel great." He even loved watching her eat as she picked through her potatoes and ate tiny tidbits of her bacon. "You going to leave that bacon?"

She set her fork down and closed her eyes briefly before she continued. "We have to talk, Morgan."

His heart sunk to his knees. Had he made a huge miscalculation?

"I need to know how to play this. J.J. said I wasn't to change my routine when I got home, but with Gibril, I honestly don't think he's involved in any way, and he's really just a friend now. With what happened last night between us, I need some boundaries."

Of course she did. He was a fool not to bring it up first.

"How close were you? I mean, any promises? Have you met his family, anything like that? And how deeply involved do you think you should be?" He tried to ask it in a way she didn't feel pressured, focusing on Gibril rather than himself.

Halley stumbled a bit, and he could see she was on uncharted ground.

"We'd sort of cooled it this past Sunday. He was asking me about what I wanted to do in my future. But we hit a bump in the road when he asked me if I wanted children some day."

Morgan knew it was a thin rope he was walking on.

"What did you tell him?" He held his breath because he knew if Gibril had asked her about children, he was serious about her. He was fairly sure she'd already picked that up.

"I told him I never thought about it, because I was having too much fun with the business, and that was a completely honest answer."

"So what was the problem? I can understand that."

"The problem is that he was used to women who felt it was a higher calling or something to bear children and stay at home. Frankly, it shocked me he should have such a provincial point of view. It's the only time I've heard him suggest that perhaps this work of mine wasn't what I really should be doing, like he knew better than I did. I could see there was no future."

Morgan could watch her talk for hours. When she began to tear up, he grabbed her hand from across the table. "Hey, hang in there. I know this is all confusing as hell. You're doing great."

"And then there's you," she whispered, still holding his hand.

Morgan rose and stood beside her. "Come here, Halley."

She scrambled to her feet and then fell into his arms. This sweet, beautiful, powerful creature had wrapped her arms around him like he was her lifeline. He felt so wonderful he could hardly speak.

"Halley. We don't have to talk about us, yet, if all this is too much."

He could feel her nodding against his chest.

"I don't want to rush things, but just know that I am here. I've always been here, and I'm not leaving."

She sniffled and wiped her eyes with the backs of her hands. He grabbed a napkin for her.

"We just got to sort through all this. And," he tipped her chin up toward him, "although it would bring me great joy, we probably can't be affectionate in public, just in case. That's going to be the hardest thing for me," he admitted as he brushed his lips against hers. He ended it with a kiss to her forehead, as well. "We've got time to figure something out. Try not to worry."

They gathered their things to head downstairs. He took one last glance at the room with the disheveled bedding. The smell of her perfume and sunlight bathed everything in a golden glow, and he hoped it would be the start of something he could spend a lifetime working on, not the beautiful end to an old story. He had hope. What they shared wasn't just sex. There was lots of need, and although neither of them said it last night, there was also love.

That felt great.

MORGAN BROUGHT THE truck around and waited for her to finish checkout. When she climbed into the cab, he took her bag and noticed she had another bag from the hotel store.

"I bought you a present."

Morgan opened it to find a long-sleeved, button down white shirt with the Coronado Rose emblem stitched into the front.

"Thank you. That's a nice shirt."

"I got an XL. They have a double X, but I thought—"

"I'm not *that* big."

Her face instantly went red. She leaned over, kissed him, and whispered, "Oh yes, you are."

They quickly parted. Morgan searched the surrounding area and then turned on the engine.

"Wait! You *are* going to wear it, right?"

"I'll put it on when we get there."

"You don't like it. I'll take it back."

"No, sweetheart." And then he realized he was being a jerk. He ripped open the package, pulled out pins stuck into the collar, removed his well-used pink shirt and tossed it over the seat, and put the new shirt on. He tucked it in as best he could with the steering wheel getting in the way.

She discovered what part of his problem was and touched him in the groin, giving him a nice squeeze. He gasped.

"It's perfect. You look marvelous!" she said with a tease. "And you smell great. What are you using?"

"Your deodorant." Morgan shrugged. "Sorry."

Her laugh was fun to hear. It was so blasted wonderful to see her happy.

"Now are we ready to go?" he asked.

"Proceed to the rendezvous. Should I wear a blindfold?"

He patted her thigh. "Next time you're naked with me, sweetheart. I promise."

After a few blocks, Morgan decided to ask a couple of questions so she didn't have to answer it with the audience he was expecting at the apartment. The GPS unit was tracking their moves. The place was very close, so he had to hurry.

"Have you met any of Gibril's family?"

"One of his sisters. She doesn't wear a burqa, but she covers her head. They live on the Peninsula somewhere. He has other family in the central valley and up north. His parents are not in the U.S."

"You know anything about them?"

"His sisters married Arab men. That's all I know. They don't work, and both have children. His sister is very nice. A little shy, but nice."

"So how long have you dated?"

"Almost a year."

"How did you meet?"

She frowned and tilted her head to the side. "I can't remember—oh yes, it was at the grocery store of all places. He asked me to help him find a ripe watermelon."

"Classic bachelor pickup line. And you fell for that?"

"It led to a cup of coffee and an exchange of phone numbers, so I guess it worked."

"Only thing better than that is to stand in the baking section looking puzzled and ask a young lady what I'd need for a pie crust. They love it when you look lost."

"I'll bet." She reached over and gave him another squeeze.

"You're gonna have to stop that. We're nearly here, and I'm about to take you in the back and give you a spank and then fuck your brains out. So quit it, okay?"

She leaned forward, and he cautioned her. "No kissing, remember? You don't know who is watching."

"Let them watch."

But he held her off. "Halley, this is serious. And, by the way, you're not acting exhausted. I like that."

"I do, too."

He'd parked in the upper level of a nice looking condo complex, like J.J. had instructed. She brought her overnight bag with her that also contained her new computer. Morgan pulled it off her shoulder again as they headed for the entrance.

He checked his phone for the number and knocked on door 408.

J.J. answered it right away. Behind him were the two new recruits. As Morgan and Halley moved through the doorway, J.J. pinched Morgan's nipple near where the Coronado Rose stitching was. "Nice touch, stud."

"It was a gift. I don't want to think about it, and you shouldn't be, either."

J.J. slammed the door behind him. "Okay, this is Halley, our Wonder Woman. Halley, this is Stanley and Taylor. You guys show me how you'd greet a Muslim woman, like you did a few minutes ago."

They both started speaking Arabic, and Morgan only recognized the "As-Salam" or first part of the greeting.

"Holy cow. I got the shivers," Halley said.

"They're fluent in Arabic and have mastered several of the dialects, too. Amazing talent," added Morgan.

J.J. motioned for them to sit at the small table just off the kitchen.

"So the boys will be going up to Stockton today, snooping around, trying to get a foot into the doorway there. I'm leaving how they do it entirely up to them so I can deny anything in case something happens."

Morgan agreed. Halley was watching them closely. No doubt their young age and the danger they were getting themselves into bothered her. It bothered him.

"Taylor, Stanley, you have any questions for Halley before you leave?"

"Your boyfriend, Mr. Messi," Taylor shot a quick glance at Morgan before he continued. "Can you tell me about his family or any relatives who might have information about the mosque or the Imam?"

"I wasn't even aware of this mosque until these two told me," she answered. "If you think it would be safe, I could find a way to ask Gibril. And, by the way, he's not my boyfriend. He's a close friend."

J.J. cleared his throat. "Great," he mumbled. Morgan felt the chilling stare down and then continued to watch Halley.

"Don't ask him. I don't want anyone in the family to get their radar up," said Stanley. "The community will already be suspicious of us. I mean, look at us."

Halley smiled. "You two are very brave."

Taylor cocked his head, "Ah, it's what we were trained to do."

"These two were formerly working for Kyle's team," Morgan told her.

"You look so young."

"We like being underestimated. But it sucks with the girls," Stanley said.

J.J. inserted himself. "I think what they're saying is, if it comes up, try to learn something, just to see if there's a connection. We don't have a reason to suspect Gibril, except that he's close to you and we know you are the target. He could be an unwitting participant. Who knows? So at this point, we need to keep our eyes and ears open."

Halley nodded. "I see. I'll do what I can."

"And you didn't break it off with him, because that

would be *very* unfortunate." J.J. drilled another laser beam into Morgan's face. "I hope that didn't happen or won't happen."

"No. That didn't happen. But we're friends, just not as intimate as we once were, I think. That happened naturally over the course of the past few days on its own. He's working hard to win me back. I feel kind of sorry for him."

"Don't." J.J.'s face was completely deadpan.

"But he's a very nice man. He's done nothing but shower me with gifts and affection."

"And he could be grooming you."

"I think I can be a good judge of character, J.J. Or is it Hank now?"

Morgan felt her backbone and hackles rise. J.J. would have to be careful, or he'd get a taste of her stubbornness.

"Just be careful, Halley," Morgan said as he placed his hand on hers. "Remember, everyone is a suspect, except the people in this room. We don't know where it's going to come."

"And I have something else, Halley," J.J. began. "Your computer was fitted with a very sophisticated tracking device. There were malware links installed, giving someone access to certain emails and other things related to your business. Your computer was a portal for someone."

"So it will be suspicious for it to have been stolen," she stated.

"They're going to try to make it look like someone from a gang was trying to work on it, get your private information, and we'll watch them get locked out. If we can, we want to trace who's monitoring you, but we have to catch them live."

"Wow. Is there any possibility this could just be hackers and not something more nefarious?"

"If it walks like a duck—" Stanley started.

"It's not Bigfoot," ended J.J. "It has all the earmarks of something worse, mainly because of the tracking device. It could even be someone looking for a quick kidnapping, but to get access to your computer, well, you tell me how many people have that opportunity?"

"There would be only two, or perhaps three. Crystal, her brother—although he's never been in my home office that I know of—and Gibril."

"There you go," said Morgan.

"Your assistant, Crystal, how long have you worked together?" J.J. asked.

"About six months. My other assistant got very ill, some sort of intestinal problems, and had to move back home with her parents in Texas."

"So how did you get Crystal and then her brother?"

"Well, I think I advertised on Craig's list. She had worked for a big real estate guru and traveled with him from town to town as he sold his tapes and such. I thought she'd be perfect. No one else had those qualifications. She'd even set up events for him at big venues like Las Vegas and New York."

"Why did she quit?"

"It was one of those sexual assault cases. He couldn't keep his hands to himself. Crystal had to leave."

"You checked her references?" Morgan asked.

"Well, no, under the circumstances. But she showed me the venues, some of his organizing notes. I mean, she had a whole manual about how to do her job."

J.J. stared at the tabletop. "Pretty unbelievable, wasn't it?"

"Yes. I thought I'd been totally blessed."

"And Orestes?" Morgan asked.

"Well, her brother was former military and fresh out of the service. He worked security, she said."

"And you didn't check him out, either," asked J.J.

"No. I don't even know how you do that sort of thing. You just call up the Marines and say, 'Hey, can I have a reference?' I mean how silly would that be?"

"Nobody's faulting you, Halley. We're trying to figure out how they got in, because it's certain, someone's trying awfully hard to get you so tied up you'd be completely off guard and helpless. That's where we come in."

Morgan was glad J.J. had explained it that way, and he could feel Halley was slightly more relieved.

Morgan checked his watch. "Should I order something for lunch, or do you want me to take Halley somewhere before I run her up to the airport?"

"God, do you ever stop eating?" she asked him.

"Only when I'm not hungry."

"Up to you guys," J.J. addressed the boys.

"I think we're gonna hit the road. It's a bit of a drive, and we're packed, ready to go," said Taylor.

"You got your phones?" Morgan asked.

"Yup. Got our cash, our phones, a couple of clean tee shirts, and some good music for the road. J.J. has our numbers."

"And you have mine?" asked Morgan.

"Yup."

"One other thing, we've been lax on the J.J. vs. Hank name. After today, it's always Hank. I have a family to protect."

Morgan realized J.J. was also putting his life on the line, but families were collateral damage in cases like these if they had been overseas. He just never thought he'd have to worry about it in the U.S.

Halley summed it up well. "Thank you, all of you. You let me know what else I can do. And if I screw up, you make sure and tell me." She had squeezed Morgan's hand under the table for special emphasis.

The boys got up, as did everyone else. There was an exchange of hugs, and then it was just the three of them in the condo.

"Those kids are amazing, J.J.—Hank," Morgan corrected. "Now I know how Kyle felt sending us out on our missions."

"They're itching for it. I just hope they have the street smarts to play safe, but they're committed one hundred percent. You know what they had to go through to get on the Teams," J.J. reminded him.

"And I hope their enthusiasm makes up for their lack of real streetfighter experience," he answered. "So far, we have a good team. Now all we need is a little luck."

Halley slipped her arm around Morgan's waist and drew herself into him, allowing his body to protect her. He searched J.J.'s eyes while he experienced the most important person in the world needing and feeling safe with him. The feeling inside his chest was more than he had a right to experience. It was Heaven itself.

And J.J. saw every bit of it and nodded his acceptance.

CHAPTER 16

MORGAN HAD OFFERED to get some lunch for the three of them, but J.J. wouldn't have any of it. "Go spend a few moments, grab something, and then let's all get back to work."

Halley knew he was troubled by something, so she asked him.

J.J. stood before her and put his hands on her shoulders. "You are a strong woman, a brave and powerful woman. This guy here is as tough as they come, and he's survived a lot. Under any other circumstances, I'd be thrilled there is a rekindled romance going on here—"

Morgan had started to object.

"Nah, nah, hear me out, Morgan." He focused back on Halley. "He may not be able to focus and concentrate. It helps that you are also the person we're trying to protect, so that part is okay. But I need him lean, angry with all the blood he can spare rushing to his brain."

He was right, of course.

"So there's a part of me jumping for joy. There's another part that's saying inside, *'I hope they don't get us all killed.'* On the Teams, he would have been able to rope himself in. I know what he's feeling and thinking, because if it was my wife and kids, I'd feel exactly the same. Let's not get too caught up in the hearts and flowers. This is war. It's about survival. We have an administration to protect, a country to protect, two thousand lovely ladies to protect, and you. We have the trust and faith that we can do it. We can't be thinking about anything else."

He removed his hands, from her shoulders, stepped back, and then thought of something else.

"I don't ever want to see any handholding, kissing, or hugs, even if they look non-sexual, until this whole thing is over with. Good news is your event is only three weeks away. Bad news is, we could be wrong, and it could happen tomorrow."

"Thank you, J.J."

He got that twinkle in his eye as he squinted and angled his head just to let her know he got the inference.

"I'll do everything in my power to hold up my end of the bargain. After this afternoon, it will be war. I'll keep my wits about me. I trust you guys, all of you, and

I'll tell you what I told Morgan. I appreciate my freedoms. I can get up on stage and talk about women being powerful. There are only a few places on the planet where that is even a possibility. We have you to thank for that," she admitted.

"Thanks. Now go and get her out of your sight, Morgan, or I'm gonna fire your ass and get someone else."

She could tell Morgan was furious with the obvious reprimand, but J.J. was totally right. She had to maintain her war-like mindset, look for advantages, and not shrivel in the face of fear. She'd had her time to be completely overwhelmed with the scenario, and Morgan had been there to help her out. Now she was going to have to do it by herself. He wasn't going to be right there at her side. He'd be doing his job—something much more important than pleasuring her little ass.

Although it sure had been fun.

HE TOOK HER to a burger joint because it was fast. He ordered double on the fries, the largest size shake, and a double patty with onion rings and extra cheese. She guessed his eating was his form of dosing. If she ate that way, she'd be in a coma for a week.

She picked at her lettuce wrapped Angus burger and stole a couple of his fries. Her ice tea tasted good, but her stomach was still misbehaving. The rule had been not to show affection in public, but that didn't stop him from warming her thigh with the big muscled inside of his under the table.

They avoided looking at each other, except for quick stolen glances, mostly because she figured it was as painful to him as it was for her. J.J. was right. It would be healthier for both of them to be apart, to work out all the details without being in such close proximity.

But as the minutes ticked away, her courage failed. With her chin quivering and droplets of tears falling into her burger, the sadness filled her and her heart felt totally broken. Why couldn't they have done this sooner? Why had they missed out on those ten years? Why had she overlooked what she now saw in Morgan?

"Come on," he said after he threw his burger down and grabbed her hand. He pulled her into the women's restroom and locked the door.

This was no time for a quickie like they used to do in the old days. This was all wrong, and she started telling him this. She could barely see him through her tears.

With his fingers smelling of ketchup and burger sauce, he cupped her face in the palms of his hands and kissed her.

She tried to talk, but he had his tongue pressing against hers, his mouth devouring her breath and any possible words. His thumbs wiped away her tears when they parted. He wet a paper towel and dabbed her forehead, under her eyes, and under her chin. Her mouth tasted like his burger, including the onion rings, which she hated. She licked her lips, now able to see him at last.

"Just hold on, Halley. You can do it. J.J. is right. You're one of the most powerful women I know. You're brighter, more observant, have more heart and drive, and you're more stubborn than any Navy SEAL I've ever met. We're way out of your league."

She nodded. "Thank you," she said, but her voice sounded more like a five-year-olds. It was all she could do now.

"No regrets, Halley. Life is what it is. But for us to have a chance, we've got to do some very dangerous things. I need you sharp and solid."

"I can do that."

"I know you can. I've seen you do it tons of times."

Someone was knocking on the door.

"Just a minute," they both said in unison. Halley slapped her hand over her mouth and made a face.

"I'm sure they've seen it before. Are you better now?"

"Yes. Thank you."

"You can do this, Halley. Look, if I have to live with the images of you and Mr. Sheikh having a romantic dinner or imagine what he's doing when he's next to you or perhaps kissing you—"

"No, Morgan. I can't do that."

"But you *have* to. I'll be the first one to shake his hand and apologize if we've been wrong about him. But you know it's important for you to play along."

"I know. So I can get naked and dance on tables for him, then?"

Morgan growled. "Not. Funny."

"Can I do this?" She squeezed his package and ran her tongue over his lips, first the upper, then the lower. "Or this?" She took his hand and slipped it up under her short skirt and into her panties.

"None of that. Don't even think about that. It's forbidden."

His fingers were exploring her sex and making her hot.

She whispered in his ear. "Put it in one more time, Morgan. Just once more."

Again, the sound of banging on the door made the whole room shake, but Morgan had moved aside the elastic of her panties and had his cock inside her. She stepped on the toilet seat to bring herself up for better angle. Watching his blue eyes, she felt the warm, fat shaft of his find its way home.

"Not very romantic," he whispered.

"Should we wait until the manager unlocks the door?"

But then they heard keys. Morgan pulled out quickly, and she flattened her skirt. They opened the door and dashed down the hallway back to the dining room. A line of people had been waiting to use the rest room.

She didn't look at anyone's face, but ducked and followed the direction his beefy hand was leading her.

Inside the cab of the truck, Morgan squeezed the steering wheel. "Fuck, Halley. You're going to be the death of us both. I'm not going to touch you." He held his palms up as if she was radioactive.

"Fine," she said and faced the windshield, a smirk on her face. He always used to hate it when she said *fine,* because most of the time things were not fine at all, but very messed up. She'd had her last bit of fun, got him to cross the line again. Now it was time to get serious. And now she could.

"Unbelievable," he muttered while he tore out of the parking lot.

AT THE GATE, he let her off at the curb, handing her the bag she'd carry on her shoulder.

"Safe journeys, Halley. You may not see me, but if it's safe, we'll talk. Please keep in touch with J.J. or me if anything at all comes up. I'll give you updates if and when I can. But please be smart and safe."

"Yessir."

They chanced another last long look, and this time, she managed to keep her eyes dry.

"I will be missing you, Morgan."

"And you know right now what I'm doing to you in my mind," he smiled. "Now go kick some ass and take no prisoners, kid."

"Roger that. We're going to make it count." Halley used her own line for the send off.

"Make it count, indeed."

She turned and, without touching him or gesturing in any way, stepped into the terminal and didn't dare look back.

The plane ride seemed short and didn't give her nearly enough time to collect her thoughts. She had been thinking about how to work on her event, knowing that perhaps someone was out there ready to take it all away from her. While it made her angry, she knew the anger would color her decision-making.

When the plane landed, she texted Gibril, letting him know she was on the ground. She tried calling Crystal, but again only got her voicemail. She had Orestes' phone number in her old phone, and she blamed herself for not trying him sooner.

The driver was there as usual.

"Welcome home, Miss Hansen. You had a good trip?" he asked.

"It was a sad one. My friend is dying. I should be getting the text any time now."

"I'm so sorry. So this was your last time to see him?"

"Her. Friend from my past."

"Well, that's too bad. Glad you're back home. It will be good to sleep in your own bed. That's my favorite thing to do when I come home from a trip."

"You have that right. I need to catch up on my sleep."

"You have no bags?" he said as he glanced over at the carousel.

"Nope, just this one."

He opened the back passenger door for her, and she slid in, dragging her bag with her.

"I'll get that." The driver tried to put it in the front seat next to him. She pulled it back to her lap.

"No worries. I've got things to look through on the way home, but thanks."

Every little deviation from their normal routine was a red flag for her. He'd never been so talkative. His usual nature was pure stoic.

She also felt his eyes on her, watching her from the rear view mirror from time to time. Had he always been this interested?

She made a mental note to look over her driver contract and perhaps have J.J. and the guys check out the firm that hired the drivers out. They usually sent this guy, but there were also two others they used. Up until now, there hadn't been an issue. Now, everything had changed.

They arrived at her first gate, and she retrieved the clicker and opened the gate. She wondered why she'd never given the driver her codes, like she had the landscapers, but she'd had the little crew of workers now for over five years and she's trusted them from day one. Gibril had suggested she get a driver so she wouldn't have to trudge the dark parking lot at SFO by herself when she came home, and since she could afford it, she agreed. It also gave her time to call everyone who needed to know she was back in town.

So now there was a very distant connection between Gibril and the limo company. She would ask him if by chance he used the same car service.

She thanked him, gave him his usual hundred dollars, and retired for the night. Pulling the computer from the bag, she plugged it in at her office to let it fully charge before starting it up again.

She fixed an ice water in the kitchen and clicked on the news. There was some political reporting and a follow-up on the Portland killings, which she'd all but forgotten. Weather was going to be clear all week.

She wasn't hungry, so she shut down the lights in the office after checking all the doors and windows downstairs and the deadbolt on the front door. The housekeeper had been in to clean yesterday so everything looked in good order.

She slipped off her shoes and climbed the stairs to her bedroom, bringing the rest of her weekend bag. She emptied and sorted the dirty clothes, added things to the cleaner's bin, placed her cosmetic pouch back on the hook in her closet, put her hair up in a clip, and stepped into the shower.

Afterward, she noticed she'd missed a call from Gibril. Tucking herself into the covers, clean and with a clean flannel nightie for this chilly night, she dialed him back.

"Aw, I am so sorry for you, Halley. You must be exhausted and panicked," he said.

"I don't understand."

"Your friend and then your computer. How are you ever going to get by without all your information?"

"I'm hoping they'll find it. I've called the lost and found at SFO several times, but—"

"Oh, so you lost it at the beginning of your trip."

"I was so distracted. I rushed to catch a flight."

"Halley, are you sure you wouldn't like some company? I can be a very good shoulder to cry on."

"Oh, you're so sweet, Gibril, but I'm going to turn

in early and try to pick up the pieces tomorrow. It will be a hard day."

"Again, so sorry. Now, what can I do? I insist."

She tried to laugh and sound gracious, but his persistence was annoying her.

"I just need the time to reflect on things, meditate. I haven't been able to do that for two days now, and I need it."

"Then do it tonight."

"That's a very good idea. I think I will! Thank you, Gibril. And how is everything with you?"

"We've been in several high-level meetings for these past two days. Very close to funding a really big venture."

"That's awesome. Are you point man?"

"Hardly. But I introduced the two sides together, so it's partially mine."

"Never a bad thing to make brownie points with the boss, is it? Well, I'll let you get to bed yourself. I'll ring you tomorrow after I've had a chance to sort my to-do pile."

"Yes, I'll look forward to that. Good night, sweet Halley. May the stars rock you to sleep and bring you a hundred years of refreshment."

"That was lovely. Another thousand-year-old poem?"

"Indeed. Rest well, and we'll talk in the morning."

After they hung up, Halley considered reading one of her romance novels, but with the memories of her past two days still fresh, she didn't want to alter her dreams with another hero.

She turned off the lights and slid down, hearing the quiet, all alone in her big bed with the expensive sheets scented with lavender. It used to feel so lush and opulent.

Now she felt like a young princess from a fairy tale, locked in a castle and all alone. Waiting.

But she opened her eyes and stared at the ceiling and realized she wasn't waiting. She was resting, garnering her courage and her energy.

Tomorrow, she would do battle. And if the hero showed up in this story, that would be all the better.

CHAPTER 17

MORGAN AND J.J. decided to take a field trip to the Grand Fordham in San Jose to check out the venue. Halley had told them she was using the security staff from the hotel, which was usually how it was done. They wanted to snoop around and perhaps talk to them under the guise of wanting to put on a rock concert at the auditorium.

"I think we should take a visit to our friend Gibril's office, too. What do you think?" Morgan asked.

"Both of us?"

"Wouldn't it be more plausible? Perhaps ask him how the start-up was done. Say we'd invented something we needed help with."

"I don't think it works that way, but we can try."

On the way up, they brainstormed several companies they could say they were seeking venture capital money for. After much back and forth, they found the right one.

At the Grand Fordham, they were met in the lobby by Jason Kalolo, the hotel's Samoan head of security. He looked more like he belonged on a wrestling tag team, with arms twice the size of Morgan's and knuckles that very nearly did drag on the ground. His stubby legs were hidden under the black uniform he wore, but the former SEALs knew he was probably fast as the wind with deadly accurate kicks.

"I got the venue all worked out here, Bro," he said when they asked to see a sample of how they'd set a big event up. He'd taken them to his office, a small cubicle around the corner from the reception desk. He stood in front of a huge post-it note, a diagram of the property set up in the middle, and exits noted, as well as assignments made for manning them. "These are my men."

"Will they be armed?"

"Not allowed in the city limits. We'll have pepper spray, and we plan on interfacing with some San Jose PD, who will be armed. We'll be in constant radio communication. A couple of my guys are also on the force."

"So this is for over a thousand attendees?" Morgan pretended.

Jason checked the center of the building, putting his finger on the icon. "Says 2400. That's capacity for this room."

"What happens if you get more attendees?" asked J.J.

"Not likely. Fordham Corp. is not too keen on losing their license to operate these events. We got a city fire Marshall, a woman, and she's a ball buster."

Perfect, thought Morgan.

"So how do you control crowd size, and how do you run security behind stage?" J.J. asked.

"Normally, the musician provides that. We'll interface, of course, and always have two uniforms there. That's part of the fee you'd pay in advance, because sometimes we're paying time and a half to the off-duty police who volunteer, but it's still overtime, and they get the free show from stage side."

"How do you know who's legit?"

"You can issue a backstage pass, or just have one of your crew only let in certain people. That's the way it's usually done with concerts." He slapped the sticky paper with the back of his hand. "She doesn't have anyone like that, so we're providing the beef, except for a few people she personally wants to include."

They determined the crowd was not processed with a metal detector, that it had to be requested, and Halley hadn't done so.

"So what kind of music do you guys play?"

"Rock, heavy metal. We do some tribute things," said J.J.

"So I haven't heard of you then?"

"Not likely," they both said in unison.

"I'd like to take a look at the auditorium and the stage, if we could," Morgan asked.

"Sure thing. Follow me." Jason led them to one of a series of four double doors all labeled A through D. *Oracle Auditorium* was spanned above all four sets of doors in foot high, gold letters. The Samoan pulled on the first set and found it locked. He tried the second one and had more success.

Morgan was shocked that the auditorium wasn't fully secured. Inside, Jason turned on the house lights, and two huge amber-colored chandeliers lit up, sending a warm glow over the sloped floor and light tan cushioned seats. The stage was farthest away, circular-shaped, elevated about five feet, and extending out into the audience so that a performer could nearly work in the round. There were a couple sets of stairs at each side.

As they made their way to the front, a small piece of crepe paper or tissue floated to the canvas floor from above.

"What's that?" he asked.

"We have balloons, confetti, you know, anything you want, really. Most bands like streamers and glitter squares, but it's up to you."

"So the renting party has to designate what they

want then?" asked J.J.

"You have the facilities to package all these things up?"

"No, sir. We hire that out. They have a crew who work the whole bay area, including the sports teams. They come in here the day before and set it up. Part of the fee. We call her our *confetti lady*. Terrific gal."

J.J. looked to the ceiling and could make out clear plastic bags filled to bursting with pink and white balloons. "So you're ready for your next release, then? When does this one kick off?"

"Yes, tomorrow night. They loaded these up this morning. There's a shoot they throw their bags through up top above the rigging for balloons. All the tethers are tied together until the drop. They yank out the plastic as the balloons are released. Easy as pie. For the confetti, she uses her canons."

"Can I speak with her directly about what my options are?" J.J. continued.

"Well, normally people go through us. I mean, you can't schedule anything except through the hotel, but I guess she'd talk to you about what they use. Is that what you mean? They aren't going to use something that isn't cleared by us first," said Jason.

"Of course."

"I'll get you her card when we stop by my office."

Morgan couldn't believe how many unsecure places there were that someone could sneak in and cause havoc. Even backstage, there was a rear roll-up loading door that didn't even have a lock on it, if someone knew to just yank on the outside handle.

They completed their tour, declining to book a date for their rock concert. They promised Jason a follow-up visit.

Morgan surprisingly got an appointment with the Focus Forum, under the guise of seeking capital for their farming operation. He was hoping to get to see Gibril himself and asked for him in person.

The chrome and glass building was just down the street from several other icons of Silicon Valley. The two former SEALs entered the lobby and waited on brightly colored fabric cubes, scattered like jacks on the granite tile floor. They didn't have to wait long.

Mr. Messi himself greeted them and signed them in. Morgan watched his slim physique, his long delicate fingers, and his stunningly handsome dark features, and it created in him a personal storm he worked hard to control. He was dressed in an expensively tailored dark blue suit with, of all things, a red, white, and blue tie. It burned him no end. What he really wanted to do was squeeze the life out of him, slowly, strangle him with that tie. But, like he told J.J., he was there to see if the man could incriminate himself.

And then he'd strangle him.

They were taken to the elevator. "So you are in the farming business. Is this in California, or elsewhere? I detect a southern accent," he said with a dashing smile and a sweetness just under the gay-dar range. He pressed the sixth floor button with flourish, showing off his white cuffs and expensive gold cufflinks.

J.J. spoke up first. They'd talked about Morgan being the lead with the questions, but he sensed J.J. understood he was having to swallow his tongue. He made a mental note to himself to stop fisting his hands, a surefire giveaway of his deepening anger. If he wasn't careful, he'd start stuttering or drooling and make a fool of himself.

"Actually, Mr. Messi—"

"Please, call me Gibril." The man's smile was wide and confident. There wasn't an ounce of condescension anywhere. Morgan thought his acting abilities were amazing.

"Gibril," corrected J.J., "We're setting up a marijuana collective and are planning to use state-of-the-art Dutch greenhouses. The marijuana industry will be booming in California, Colorado, and elsewhere."

"Already is," Gibril responded.

The doors opened to several offices with only glass partitions. There were no privacy walls of any kind. Only half of the offices were populated. Salesmen with headsets and stand-up desks were hard at work.

They were shown to Messi's private office, and the glass door was closed. Within seconds, an attractive secretary brought a tray of fruit, cheeses, and an array of bottled waters, all chilled, ice in etched glasses with the Focus Forum logo on them. Messi's desk was spotless. It contained a silver tray, probably his inbox, Morgan thought, with nothing in it. The black blotter his folded hands sat on was without a smudge or scratch.

His erect posture, as he leaned toward them, told them he was ready for their pitch. He didn't ask. He just smiled.

J.J. cleared his throat and managed a frown in Morgan's direction.

"Well, we have optioned a plot of land in the town of Lodi. We like the weather, and we think we can work with the town fathers without too much drama."

"I understand," Messi said.

Morgan was examining photographs on a glass credenza to Messi's back. He spotted Halley's picture from one of her events, her headset atop her head, her hands gesturing, while rose petals were being showered all around her. It was a fabulous picture, and Morgan understood how she felt, doing what she was doing at the time the shot was taken.

As J.J. and Gibril chatted back and forth, Morgan also scanned the other photographs set in crystal frames of family, groups of his colleagues in front of the Forum building, and a large gathering of what must have been a wedding party. It didn't take him long to spot the distinct white turban of an Imam who looked a lot like Al-Moustafa. He returned to target Messi and gave him a hard stare.

"Um, feel free to fill in the blanks here, Jeff," J.J. said to him with a scowl. He smiled at Messi, but Morgan could see it was one of those sickly sweet ones. "My partner here, I think, is in awe of your beautiful surroundings. He's normally very talkative."

"Ah. Well, coming to a venture capitalist firm in the first place can be intimidating. You have worked hard on your little project—"

Morgan began to growl with the sound of the word *little*. He was pretty sure he could own the word big, and there wasn't anything Gibril could do about it. Genetics.

J.J. turned to him in panic. "Are you alright, *Jeff*?"

All eyes were on Morgan. He didn't want to stare at the photographs to give himself away, but he couldn't help it.

"Pretty lady," he croaked, pointing to Halley's picture. He felt like a five-year-old with messed pants. He would thank J.J. for putting him on the spot later.

"Oh yes, she's a very close personal friend. Halley Hansen. She does women's empowerment events and seminars. Very talented."

"Very pretty, too. Your girlfriend?" Morgan's voice broke like he was fifteen.

He heard J.J. gasp next to him and, from the corner of his eye, saw him grab a handful of grapes and then throw one at him.

"So we're gonna ruin this guy's nice office with a food fight?" Morgan barked.

"I'm just saying that wasn't an appropriate question, *Jeff.*" J.J. made his eyes full and round as if to say *what the hell's the matter with you, Morgan?*

"No, please, please. Do not trouble yourselves. We are an open book here. If I didn't want you to see this lovely picture," he picked it up and handed it to Morgan, who nearly dropped it on the tile floor, "I wouldn't have put it there to be seen. She's a very special lady to me, but, sadly, I cannot call her my girlfriend. She's rather independent, and we are both playing the field. But I love being around her charm, and her charisma is off the charts."

Morgan found that his jaw had dropped, and he was about to drool. The picture in his hand felt like a hot coal. He returned it to Gibril immediately and adjusted his seat, crossing his legs.

"If I could bottle or invent what she has, I'd be a rich man," Gibril added.

It was an odd comment, but Morgan sized him up

as genuine. He didn't overplay his relationship, and it agreed with what Halley had told them. Morgan began to see a bit of what Halley had seen in him and thought perhaps, maybe he was an honest man. But just maybe.

"Wow, that's nice. We don't run across much of that in our farming business, do we, *Jeff*?" J.J. was trying to prime the pump and get him to talk. He knew that. He hated him for it, too. So he pushed himself forward.

"So, Mr. Messi—"

"Ah! Ah! I insist. Gibril, please."

Fucking idiot.

"Gibril." He thought about screaming how many times he'd fucked her and made her come. He wanted to see the expression on this man's face when he told him that. But maybe later.

J.J. interceded. "You know what, Jeff? I can see you're having a bad day. Gibril, perhaps we could come back later?"

"Sure."

"No. I'm fine, *Hank*." Morgan saw Gibril confused, looking between the both of them, with a brittle smile, sitting back in his chair, with his fingers tented, gently resting on his slim thigh. He waited.

"Do you know anything about farming?" Morgan asked.

Behind Halley's picture, Gibril again smiled. "As a

matter of fact, I have family in the business, although they don't grow marijuana."

"Really? Where?"

"Well, actually not far from Lodi. They're in Modesto. I think it's about an hour-plus away? On the other side of Stockton from your location.

"A big farm?"

"Yes, family-owned and mostly family-run. Owned by my uncles and other family. They raise fresh vegetables for supermarkets. I doubt they'd ever get into the marijuana business. As you might guess, we are not originally from the U.S. and the use of drugs is frowned upon in our culture of origin."

It was the first time Morgan had heard that term.

"But not for you?" Morgan pressed. "I mean, are you saying you can't help us, then?"

"Oh, I'm saying nothing of the kind. Excuse me if I gave you the wrong impression. But if you're more comfortable working with someone else, I'd be happy to refer you to—"

"No, that won't be necessary," J.J. blurted out. "We're at the preliminary stage, and we want to know how it all works. We have a certain amount of capital, but for the right investor, in a budding market trend, sorry for the pun, we thought investing in our company would be lucrative. And it would give us the chance to expand faster, to take advantage of the new marijuana laws before the whole world jumps in."

"Oh, I understand completely. And I personally have no problem with it. I probably shouldn't have mentioned it. I apologize." He replaced Halley's picture on the credenza where it had been previously. He sported his biggest smile yet. "In my own defense, I just wanted to say I understand farming because of my family's enterprise."

"Of course," answered J.J.

"Is that some of your family there?" Morgan asked, pointing to the photograph.

Messi stared at him for a second before swiveling in his chair and picking up the wedding photograph. "Yes." He didn't offer to show it to Morgan, but both of them could see that the Imam was indeed Al-Moustafa. J.J. took in a quick burst of air, but otherwise didn't react.

"Beautiful family," Morgan whispered.

"Thank you. One of my nieces. I have about fourteen."

"That's a lot of weddings," J.J. remarked.

Gibril shook his head. "Indeed."

The rest of the conversation squared on logistics, how Gibril found investors, and how they worked up their report. He said he'd want to see their operation, as it was, and get more statistics on their business, what their business model was, the equipment they'd need, and a brief bio of their backgrounds, including their education.

He pushed a silver folder across the desk. "All our company information is here, along with the information we'd require to determine if we are a perfect fit and if we can help you. Fee structures, of course, are negotiable and dependent on the amounts of capital needed and raised. When were you looking to begin your buildings?"

"As close to the beginning of the year as possible," said J.J. "We have temporary hoops at other locations we've leased, but not a permanent, permitted location."

"I see, well, not sure that gives us much time, then. But why don't you look this over, fill out the paperwork and the documents we're asking for, and then come back. I promise I'll start working it up the day I receive it. Fair enough?"

They shook hands, and instead of accompanying them down to the lobby, he showed them the way to the elevator. The silver folder Morgan had in his iron grip was mangled by the time they got to the lobby.

J.J. had taken a deep breath.

"Save it until we're outside, sport," whispered Morgan, who smiled at the receptionist.

J.J. stomped his way to the truck.

"Hold it just a little while longer, *Hank*. I gotta get out of this parking lot and get some air.

"I need a fuckin' drink, and I don't drink this early in the day. You asshole, you almost tipped our hand completely."

"I know he's our link. Not sure if he's involved, but I'll bet damn sure his family is. We gotta get the boys to Modesto. Maybe split them up?"

J.J. crossed his arms. "You sure have a nose for stirring things up. I'll hand you that."

"Isn't that what we're here for, J.J.?"

"No, we're here to—"

"To gather information. This gives us lots of stuff we can tell Lambert about. I should have asked him the name of the family farm."

"It was in the report, remember?"

Morgan didn't remember that detail. "The name?"

"I'll ask Lambert. Where to now?"

"Can I see Halley?"

"Absolutely not. We've talked about this. Give her a call. I'm more inclined to go see the boys."

"I wouldn't touch that. They're just getting started. Leave them alone. They'll be checking in. In the meantime, I think we need more bodies here in San Jose. Something is definitely going on."

As J.J. made the call to Washington, Morgan was amazed they'd learned so much in such a few short days. His whole world had changed on multiple facets. It was almost like he was gluing the pieces of his life back together.

CHAPTER 18

H ALLEY ROSE EARLY to tackle the day. Crystal was still not answering her phone. She wanted to ask Morgan if he could retrieve Orestes phone number, but decided to wait until they updated her. He'd promised a phone call.

By eight, she was at her desk, working on checking her new gmail account. She notified all her credit accounts and vendors she regularly did business with online. She posted a FB post about getting ready for the big event.

The morning was overcast. As promised, Gibril called her.

"You sound much better today, Halley. Must have been some much-needed rest. Grieving can wear a person out."

"I agree."

"You've probably got lots to catch up on, but can I help you out in any way?"

"I can't find Crystal. If you could find her, that would be awesome. I have things for her to do. I fear I may have scared her away."

Gibril chuckled. "Sorry. You know I know nothing about her. But we have a couple of part-timers here I could maybe lend you. What do you think?"

Halley didn't want anyone she didn't know at this point.

"Thanks, but I'm fine. I can do everything. It will just take me longer, and now I'm behind."

"Well, save a little energy for me, okay? How about dinner? You need to be pampered."

It did sound nice, and she also wanted to do some low-level probing for the team. "I probably should work straight through dinner, but I'm going to take you up on it."

"Wonderful. I'll pick you up, say, at seven? That work for you?"

"Perfect. Thanks, Gibril."

"If you need anything else, please call me."

"I will."

Halley worked on her script for the next two hours. Then she watched some videos on how to use some of the new features on her computer. A little after noon, she got a call from Crystal.

"What's going on? I haven't heard back from you in days." Halley wasn't going to let her return without an explanation.

"I'm sorry, but I'm afraid I'm not going to be able to continue as your assistant."

"Okay. Is everything alright?"

"It's not your fault. I did take offense, but when I started thinking about things, I'm not cut out for this. You've taught me a lot, Halley. But it's time to start doing something else, not live in someone else's shadow."

"I can support that, but you understand this leaves me in the lurch for the big event? Timing's pretty crappy. I'm sorry I snapped at you, but I have to have some personal life. You do understand that, don't you?"

"I do now." She sighed. "I'm sorry I didn't let you know with better timing. Just wanted you to understand I appreciate everything you've done for me."

Halley wondered if Crystal had an inkling of what the special task force was working on. Could she be staying away for that reason?.

"Is there something else you're not telling me?"

"What do you mean?"

"Is there another reason you've been absent?"

After a long pause, Crystal confided in her that she thought she had a stalker. "Someone's been in my house while I'm at work. I got home on Monday and nearly caught someone rummaging through my things."

"Did they take anything?"

"They took an old laptop. Not one I bring to work. I had that one with me. Just my laptop. I spent Tuesday changing all my passcodes. By Tuesday night, Orestes and I had talked, and, well, we decided to move back down to Southern California. He's got a job in security on one of the movie lots. I'll find something."

"I'm sorry. Can't be anything connected to me, or is that what you're saying?"

"I don't know. But I've been feeling someone has been spying on me."

"I've felt the same thing, Crystal." Halley was being truthful, at least.

"When you left the message that your computer had been stolen, too, well, I just knew my brother and I'd made the right decision. Do you think we're being targeted for anything, Halley?"

"I was going to ask the same thing of you. But no." She hated to lie, but it was important not to reveal anything J.J. or Morgan had told her. Maybe it would be easier to have one less person to worry about if Crystal were gone. "I'll need the sales files, the data from the recent signups. Can you please send them to my new gmail account and a copy of the sales drafts to my bookkeeper?"

"Judy's already got them. But I'll forward your stuff

this afternoon." She hesitated again. "I'm really sorry. I hope everything goes well, and please call me if you have any questions about anything."

"Thanks."

She gave Crystal her new account information, asked where she wanted her and her brother's check sent, and requested she get in touch when she got situated down in Los Angeles.

Several minutes later, the recent sales updates were in her inbox, and Halley confirmed with her bookkeeper that the files had already been downloaded to her two days prior. And yes, she could see, the event was indeed sold out.

Morgan did call. She let him know about Crystal, and then he mentioned meeting Gibril.

"You did what?"

"We came up for something else, and—"

"And where are you now?"

The phone was silent at first. "I can't come see you, Halley. You know that. I'm with J.J. We're going back tomorrow. Have a couple task force guys coming out to give us a hand, based on some information we found today."

"So you'll have an update for me tomorrow, then?" she asked.

"We've started searching into several strings at the moment. Just continue to act like everything's normal."

"Is the event still on, then?"

"At this point, we're still trying to determine. If we can get inside fast enough, well, our goal is to stop them, not you."

"So what did you think of my boyfriend?" she teased.

"Are you sure he's not gay?"

"Very funny."

"He's handsome, I'll give you that. But see if you can get more information on his relatives. I think there's a link there we need to check out."

"Okay. So I'll talk to you tomorrow?"

"Yes, dear."

"You better think of something better than that to say to me next time."

"I promise," he said and then hung up.

At seven on the dot, Gibril was at the house, looking as handsome as ever. He took her to a new Italian restaurant.

"Nice thing about this one is that people haven't discovered it yet. We have space," he said as they both surveyed the half-empty dining room.

Halley looked for opportunities to ask him questions, like she was supposed to. It was difficult to get him off the subject of her "friend" in LA who had now died of cancer.

"So I finally heard from Crystal. She's not coming

back."

She watched as his expression turned serious. "Really? Why?"

"It was difficult to get exactly what was going on with her, but she claims to have been followed."

Gibril showed no expression, no reaction.

"Anyway, she and Orestes are moving back to LA. We said our good-byes. I really liked her."

"That's so odd. What will you do?"

"Perhaps I don't need one. This isn't the right time to train anybody new. I've got too much going on. The good thing was that she was so organized I'm pretty set up, and what isn't done is easily identified. She left me in good shape. It's just the emotional support I don't have."

That got Gibril's attention.

"You want me to send one of our girls over?"

"No. Like I said, I'm fine for now. But next month, perhaps we can discuss it further."

He reached for her hand. "You know I'd love to be part of that emotional support for you."

Her first reaction was to withdraw her hand, but she held firm, smiled, and thanked him. "You've already done so much."

"I've said it before. Nothing is too good for you."

"I appreciate your confidence in me. New challenges bring new opportunities, right?"

"Exactly." He held up his glass.

Halley decided to take a different tactic. She was feeling a little sad she'd been playing such a ruse on him.

"In your experience, since you are from a different culture—"

"Some claim we're from a different time zone. A throwback. You've said so yourself."

She completely agreed. "I'm sure there are many things about your culture that work."

"Have for centuries. We are a very old culture, made up of many peoples and lands. Even the religion is multisided and sometimes fractured. It is more difficult to deal with the old, very old ways."

"Yet you were able to overcome it. Look at what you've done, Gibril. It's one of the reasons I think we are such good friends."

The words were coming straight from her heart.

"I appreciate that. And you represent your culture well. You are a product of your upbringing, just as I am."

"So how do I get more of the women of your world to become involved in my seminars? Do you have any idea?"

He sat up straight, wiped his lips with the linen napkin carefully, and searched her face.

"You wish to do this?"

"I've thought about it. I know there are women who want to take control of their own lives, be less dependent on the men for their existence."

"I'll have to think about that."

She had to ask him. "What *do* you think about that? Do you see it as a good thing, a good skill for a woman to have?"

"If it's not taken too far."

"Explain."

"Halley, why all these questions all of a sudden? You've never been interested in those aspects of my culture."

"But, Gibril, can it be done? Can I reach them?"

She was relieved with his casual answer. "I suppose it can be done. Do you have another couple of hundred years? Old cultures take a long time to change. I cannot judge what I don't understand, and I don't understand much of all this hatred and violence. It comes from all places in the world, and none of it is helpful. Some don't want to change. Sometimes, we have to be patient. Enjoy those we don't agree with or don't understand for what they are, not what they are not. If we desire to live in peace, that is."

She leaned in and took his hand this time. "But I really want to know, do you think it would be a good thing?"

He stared at their fingers entwined. His dark eyes and long eyelashes swept up to meet her gaze. "Anything, Halley, that you suggest would be a good thing for anyone, man or woman. You tell people to believe in themselves, to listen to themselves. That's the best advice anyone can have."

Her eyes filled with tears. She'd been right about him. He was an innocent. A handsome, powerful, caring, innocent man. And he believed in her.

"Thank you, I'm flattered."

"You own it. That compliment is yours and yours alone. I don't say such things I don't mean."

"So how do you negotiate that with those of your family who may not agree with that opinion?"

He withdrew his hand to his lap and studied her. "I don't check out the weeds in their garden. I hope that they don't come over to pull the weeds in mine. They say fences make good neighbors. In this case, I'd say that's true."

She thought about his niece.

"Your niece coming to the seminar, will it ruffle any feathers then?"

He tilted his head, rolled his eyes as if searching the top of his skull for an answer. "I'm not sure how she negotiates that. She asked me to introduce the two of you. I know she's modern, doesn't cover herself, and wants to go to Stanford. What my uncle thinks about it, I cannot say."

"But she's the first of perhaps several who might be interested?"

"I'm not very close with my uncle. I didn't even know Fatima wanted to attend the University until she told me herself. I was surprised. So I'd doubt if my uncle's family is lining up to buy tickets, sweet Halley. As much as I'd like to tell you yes, I'm afraid I'm not the person to ask."

She understood more than he realized.

"Does any of this help?" he asked.

Her smile was genuine. She was relieved and fully convinced he had no connection to any plot to plan a terrorist attack. It just wasn't in his nature, nor could she see him having any such thoughts. Ever.

"Thank you, Gibril. Once again, you have exceeded my expectations."

"My goodness. I had no idea it was so important to you."

She finished her entree and declined another bottle of wine. She was feeling slightly tipsy from the two glasses she'd had. But she agreed to entertain dessert.

After their order was taken, she asked him about his day.

"Oh, I had the most delightful meeting with a couple of real characters. I'm not allowed to divulge the details, but, Halley, you would have loved them."

"Really?

"I do hope they come back. I'd enjoy working with them." He winked at her and whispered, "I think they're gay."

CHAPTER 19

COMMANDER LAMBERT SENT a force of operatives recently off a dark ops mission in Yemen to San Jose. Morgan and J.J. tasked them with taking over the security detail at the event center without Jason knowing anything about it. It was a tricky maneuver, but one of them planned to talk his way in as a new hire, and once they had that guy in, the rest would be able to follow.

All this was predicated on the event not being cancelled, but Morgan warned everyone, that's what they'd do, if it looked too risky.

It would have been the easy way out, to just cancel and let part of the cell scatter or go underground for awhile, but they knew from working with these groups that a kind of inertia developed, and at a certain point, even though there was the risk of detection, some cells would go through with missions that were doomed to fail. But that wasn't what the team was counting on.

They wanted the total element of surprise, that gold statue in the sky given out for missions well done.

With security in place, Morgan and J.J. focused on the family farm in Modesto, getting back information from J.J.'s contacts at the FBI that the farm had been under a low-level watch list for years, mostly because of their use of the fertilizer chemical ammonium nitrate. Although most farming communities used it, Green Valley Produce used a lot of it—more than was commonly done. And for that, a supplier had placed them on the list. That didn't, however, keep them from buying up enough to blow up a small town.

Ammonium nitrate was the most popular bomb-making ingredient readily available in California and had been a first choice of terrorists the globe over since the seventies.

Stanley and Taylor finally checked in, which was the last piece they needed before they could return home to San Diego. Morgan had even asked if they shouldn't get a place in San Jose and ditch J.J.'s apartment in San Diego, but the Commander nixed with a gentle, "I'm not using taxpayers dollars so you can get your dick polished."

Fucking J.J. You can't keep a secret.

"So how did you do?" J.J. asked the two new recruits. He put the call on speakerphone for Morgan's benefit.

Stanley began. "Where to begin? First of all, we found his beauty parlor."

"Excuse me?" J.J. asked.

"Halley was right. He spends no less than about four hours a week getting waxed, massaged and plucked. He even gets wheat grass colonics there, too."

"At a fuckin' beauty parlor? You're kidding me," barked Morgan.

"Unlike any beauty parlor you've ever seen. There are these six feet women coming in in burqas, they walk out as men, honest to God," Stanley said with glee.

"I managed to get noticed by his holiness yesterday when I came in for an ingrown toenail that, no shit, was literally killing me," Taylor continued. "He had his personal lady attend to me. She offered to lick and wax my balls, too, which made me kind of laugh."

"You guys are having way too much fun."

"Yeah, but it's hella scary here. I mean this mosque is shut down. No one says a word. They're watching me, but we're not in," said Stanley.

"He likes me better than Stanley," Taylor inserted.

"Have you heard him speak yet?" asked J.J.

"Oh yeah. Bingo there. The guy has a hard-on for uppity women. Gave a whole hour-long message on women who let themselves get defiled by infidels. 'A good father would sacrifice his daughter if she ever did this to his family.' Sounds to me like they've had some recent problems with a couple of their female members of the congregation somewhere, and the warning were that examples will be made. That group is itching for blood. You can smell it," said Stanley.

"So it isn't much of a stretch to say that Halley is in their crosshairs, then?" Morgan found himself somewhat excited with this revelation, although it was confirmation that she was, in fact, truly in danger.

"Big time. I even found the article you had us read, with the picture cut off. It was posted on the bulletin board. A westerner wouldn't be able to read it or suspect what it said."

ON THE DRIVE back to San Diego, Morgan again brought up his idea about an apartment.

J.J. looked at him like he was a smashed bug on the bottom of his shoe. "Morgan, that's the mother of lost causes. Just forget that."

"I really don't like the idea that she's all alone."

"She has Gibril, if she needs someone. And that's why it was a very bad idea to get involved with her again."

"Maybe it was a fuck up, but her bodyguard is gone, her assistant quit, and we've already determined some of his family are involved with the Imam. She lives all by herself. We have to send someone to protect her."

"Do you honestly think this Gibril is a bad guy?"

Morgan admitted he didn't think so. Halley had perhaps been right.

"So maybe we encourage her to let him stay there, for protection."

"And that could be leading her right into a trap."

"Well, you want me to get another asset? We're stretched pretty thin," said J.J.

"She does need a new bodyguard. How about one of the female agents who can double as a bodyguard as well as a secretary?"

"I'll run it by him again. But you keep your distance in the meantime."

Over the next several days, Morgan spoke to Halley each afternoon. There hadn't been any other nasty email messages or blog comments. They cancelled all her out of town speaking engagements and instead had her doing taped segments on her iPhone to post on YouTube. She also did some small group Skype calls for her high level clients.

The task force researched more information on the infamous Stockton cleric, including the fact that his diploma from the Al-Tawhidi University was bogus. Nothing could be found about him prior to four years ago when he first came to California.

But when they did further research, they traced

him back to a radical cleric in Iraq, who was eliminated by one of the SEAL Teams nearly eight years ago. Al-Moustafa had been his star pupil.

A dossier was sent to the apartment with an attachment report from the SEAL raid. The picture was that of Al-Moustafa. The gentleman staring back at them had the same deadly eyes, but the face was pockmarked from some sort of skin condition that left weeping sores. He also had a misshapen nose from a gash across the bridge. The man was tragically ugly.

But Al-Moustafa had a beautiful younger sister, who was betrothed at age nine, in a ceremony arranged by her parents. She took up household with the cleric at age eleven and was killed defending him when the SEAL team found them.

The SEAL team had tried to spare her, thinking she was the cleric's daughter. But she was caught firing a weapon in her husband's defense.

She was thirteen years old.

"He must have had a fortune in plastic surgery. He would have fooled any face recognition software at a border crossing," remarked J.J.

"No wonder he spends time at the beauty parlor. He probably gets treatments for those sores. I'll bet they're just under that well-trimmed beard," added Morgan.

WITH ONLY FOUR days to go, they'd prepared the auditorium, replacing Jason's security detail with armed Federal agents. As a precaution, one of them gave the San Jose PD and the local Fire Department a heads-up, informing them that they'd had an unconfirmed bomb threat. That meant that emergency paramedics and other vehicles would be required to be on scene for the entire venue.

Taylor reported that on one of Al-Moustafa's visits to the parlor, a dialysis van was parked behind the building. They had photographs of him entering the van for treatments.

When Morgan reached out to the Pharmacology Department at UCLA for information on the drugs the Imam might have taken for keeping his skin disease under control, he was told a common side effect was kidney failure.

Morgan understood that a dangerous man who didn't have long to live was twice as dangerous. When the only thing to live for was to die well, the man was certainly looking to make a few lines in the history books before he was oiled, perfumed, wrapped, and buried.

The family farm operated as it always did with no discernable change in their routine. Al-Moustafa continued to preach his brand of personal hatred. Stanley befriended a new recruit who had enrolled in the local college on a student visa. But he confided in Stanley that his parents had offered him up for a secret mission for the Imam. Stanley pledged to help him any way he could, and he was told instructions would be coming before the weekend—the day of the Summit.

Agents checked with the confetti lady's crew and had someone assigned to work with them to guard the shoots above the catwalk for the release of rose petals. None of the backstage doors were allowed to remain open. J.J. was to be up top with the lighting crew while Morgan was going to be stage level, as backup protection for Halley in case the unthinkable happened.

Commander Lambert finally gave permission for Morgan to become the bodyguard for Halley when it got down to two days prior. She'd been a trooper, Morgan told him. She'd even had Gibril spend a couple of nights in her guest room, and it had helped her nerves.

Morgan knew it was too much of a risk that someone might take out the easy target, go for a kidnapping or some other sensational act against her in case their plan to foil the attack was discovered. And this close to the event, none of them wanted her to spend those nights alone or without someone they weren't one hundred percent sure of.

She was delighted when he was able to call her to let her know.

"I'll wait up for you. You can come tonight, right? Or should I pick you up at the airport?"

"I want you to stay home, safe, in one of those little pink things you have."

"Your wish is my command."

"So you better buzz me in."

"You better get here quick."

Three hours later, he was outside her gate, giving his name to the com. Five minutes after that, he was naked and in her bed.

CHAPTER 20

H ALLEY HAD A hard time believing he was finally
here with her. It had been a busy, but rough few
days. She was sensitive to both loud noises and the
little noises like tree branches scratching on the windows. Normally, she kept her windows unshuttered,
but when Morgan told her that they had a picture
taken from the East Bay showing her sitting at her
breakfast table, she became possessive of her privacy.

Now, she could let down, just a bit. And that was
exactly how she felt after his phone call. Relieved. She
was more relieved than she was happy to see him, but
she was okay with that. Being happy was going to take
time. Her stressful days had strung like heavy black
pearls. Morgan would love the coldness right out of her
bones and bring her back to life. Only he could do that.

Living in her beautiful glass house on the shining
hill had turned into a fishbowl kind of existence. She
surprised herself that she could even concentrate to

remember what day it was.

She practiced and polished her presentation, streamlined it, cut out all the unnecessary words. She pumped it up with emotional stories, things about life and color, about living with purpose, standing up for yourself and slaying the enemy of all creativity—Fear.

She did all the preparation, not knowing for sure if she'd get the chance to even get up on stage. These circumstances and all the details, she couldn't possibly control. She had to trust the heroes there to protect her: the Delta Force guys, and other specialists, including San Jose's finest police force, fire departments, and emergency first responders. All she had to do was show up and deliver. Make it count. She was going to make it the best presentation of her life.

Morgan chased her up the stairway, shedding his clothes along the way. He nearly did a cartwheel over the railing when he had to use it for balance. She loved his big, hulking frame, the muscles of his chest and shoulders that moved in beautiful symphony as he came for her, chased her, wanted her.

His return to her life was even better than the first time. The ten years they were apart seemingly enhanced and accelerated the time they now had, she thought as she rounded the doorway to her bedroom. She dove into the fresh sheets with the rose scent. And he was there too, suddenly taking command of her body, arching, pressing, pulling her into his world and sharing his passion.

He could make her bloom like no other, she thought. His long strokes were so desperately needed. She craved the smell of him and his deep growling sounds as he took everything she could give and demanded more. He touched and explored. He kneaded and found her soul, uncoiled it, and set it free.

Maybe the danger all around them heightened the miracle of their lovemaking. But the glow was back. She had come alive. When she found him again, she discovered that better version of herself. They were the perfect fit.

She felt her body shiver and release to him. Facets of Morgan she'd seen these past weeks played on the big screen in her head. She saw his face as he told her, *Do you honestly think I'd ever let anything hurt you if I was alive to stop it?* His curious choice of the pink shirt. The way he smelled using her deodorant. *I'm all revved up just in case you decide to drop that gate, sweetheart.*

His long arms pressed against hers, extended out at her sides, fingers possessing fingers, pushing her deep into the mattress with every thrust. Everything she had belonged to him. Every cell in her body needed him more the more he took her.

At last, he collapsed on top of her, his breathing matching hers until she couldn't breathe any longer with the weight of him and still she wanted him covering her wrung out body.

"Never again," he whispered and gave her space by leaning on his side and placing a palm against her upper chest, watching it rise and fall with her breath.

"Never? What do you mean?"

"I'm never going to go that long without being in your bed. I don't care if you fall in love with someone else some day, I'm staying. I'm coming along on the honeymoon."

She pulled the sheets to her chest, tucked her knees in, and laughed. It felt so good to do that.

Morgan pulled the sheets away. "You're blocking my view," he said as he laved and kissed her left nipple. She pinched his and then also turned to her side, throwing one leg over his hip. The warm air between them made the covers unnecessary. She held his head to her chest, her fingers sorting through his hair, lazily outlining the shape of his ear.

"I must have been crazy to let you go, Morgan. I still can't believe I actually let you walk away."

He looked up, kissed her. "I was just thinking that as well."

"So are you ready for the big event?"

"We've tried to think of everything. Everyone's got their eyes and ears open. We're as ready as we'll ever be."

"I am, too."

"No regrets, Halley?"

"Nope."

"We can call it off and be safe."

"Or we can go forward, make them move, and then catch them red-handed. That's what you do, Morgan. I'll dive off any cliff if I know you're there to catch me."

CHAPTER 21

G IBRIL HAD RED roses delivered to the house on Saturday morning, the day of the event. Morgan went out to the gate to pick them up and tipped the delivery girl generously.

He loved seeing Halley's perplexed expression as he brought them proudly inside, wearing only his red, white and blue frog boxers. He didn't even have shoes or slippers on. And he didn't care. He was stretching out the last few minutes they had of normalcy before the midnight HALO jump of a day it was going to be. But he was used to it. He knew J.J. and the other crew was checking everything over and over, and everyone was on standby for a call from Stanley, who was likely to be the person closest to the heart of the plan.

He focused on the scent of the roses and the little card that came with them, and stopped in front of her.

"He does this better than I do."

She didn't answer him, but smiled and plucked the

card, leaving him standing with the bouquet. Through the petals, he watched her read the note. He knew she was bittersweet about telling Gibril about their rekindling and he was going to work hard to be a decent guy and not get jealous of their friendship, if it could be preserved afterwards. He even managed to scrape up some guilt about wanting to strangle the man while shouting what he'd done to Halley in graphic detail. But that was the old Morgan. Today, everything would be between the lines.

Until all hell broke loose. And that was definitely going to happen today too.

"Can I set these down? They're kinda heavy," he pleaded.

She took them from him, turned her pretty little neck and her torso away from him, bent over and placed them on the coffee table, where the other ones had been some three weeks ago.

Her pink nightgown was pulled down over one shoulder, her blonde hair all mussed, and her eyes were drunk with what he was feeling, too. He was always recovering from sex, so he could have more sex as soon as possible.

She stepped up to him and put her arms up over his neck, which prompted him to pull her delicious ass into his hardening groin. Her head came forward, and they met in the middle. "Maybe we should just stay home and fuck. What do you say? You suppose the CIA would mind?"

Morgan couldn't hold his chuckle in. It was a seriously twisted thought. There wouldn't be a place on the planet he could hide if he did that one. That was assuming they lived to tell the tale.

"I'll be sure to put that in my report, just so they know how close we came to calling it all off. They'll definitely want to know."

She snickered and pulled herself against him, wrapping one arm around his waist and the other still up around his neck where she deliciously squeezed his aching muscle. For a few seconds, they swayed back and forth, neither wanting to be the one to pull away first.

But she did. "I guess it's showtime, Morgan, my love."

"Yup." He saw in her beautiful face that she believed in him, and he hoped to the God of Frogs that he'd be worthy, that they'd thought of everything. He didn't want to let her down. "You're amazing, Halley. Simply amazing."

"Like I said, I'll jump off any cliff if I know you'll be there to catch me."

He wouldn't tell her about his doubts. He was honest with himself about his own limitations. He didn't need to warn her about the fact that, of all the missions they'd been on, only once had everything worked out as planned. This one had still too many unknowns. But they'd done the best they could do, until it was proven otherwise. So, they had to be ready for all of them.

They both got dressed. Halley wore a form-fitting white suit. He hated to admit it sort of made her look like the sacrificial lamb. But white was her choice. They took a cab over to the Grand Fordham, because it was random and anonymous and breaking a routine, which was important for today.

The cab driver smelled of pot, which annoyed Morgan. It also annoyed him that Gibril had thought he and J.J. were gay.

"So Gibril will meet you up on stage, then? He's going to be in the wings?"

He knew this would be safe, because orders were for everyone to go through a metal detector, even the stage crew and cameraman. And there would be at least three snipers in the rafters checking out the crowd below, as well as everything behind the curtain. Halley was having the show taped for later airing. Morgan thought that was a rather bold move.

"Yes. He's meeting his niece in the audience, and then he'll join us backstage."

"What are you going to say to him when he discovers I am not really a pot farmer?"

The cabbie raised his eyebrows and peered into the

mirror at him for the remark.

"I'll let you figure that out." She opened her computer and sent her notes to the technician preparing the teleprompters. After she hit send, she took a deep breath and closed her laptop. "All done. Just in case, though, in case they screw it up, I want you to hold onto my computer."

"I'm going to have my hands full, Halley."

"We'll know right away if their system is working, and I'll take the computer back from you. Just keep it in my bag, okay?"

Of course there was no problem with this. His main job was to stay as close to her as possible, and, if need be, take the bullet for her. If Gibril was there too, he could protect the other side of her.

They arrived at the rear, passing the main entrance of the building. Crowds of women were standing on the steps, taking selfies, and hugging their buddies. Morgan was proud of the positive attitude and number of smiling faces he saw. He looked at the top of the building and noted a well-placed agent, crouching behind the concrete façade of a winged angel. He was watching the steps below with binoculars.

Morgan paid the cabbie and escorted Halley through the service entrance. He recognized the look of the Delta Force guy who opened the door for them.

"Thank you for being here," he said.

"Just doin' my job. Thanks for having me. You look wonderful, Miss Hansen."

Halley smiled and gave him a peck on the cheek.

"There. Don't say I never gave you anything," Morgan whispered.

A hotel representative showed Halley to the green room for her makeup. A red bouquet of roses waited there as well. "I see a pattern here."

"He knows I love roses. Read me the card," she said as she got up into the makeup artists chair and let her begin.

The envelope was sealed, and the handwriting was very small. "You lead women to—" Morgan had to stop. This was a threat.

Halley instantly sat up and brushed the artist to the side. "What did you say? That's the same as the email I got."

"I'm not reading this to you. You don't need it. But I'm calling J.J. and have to get it to him."

"No. Don't leave me. You get someone else to deliver it," Halley demanded. "Before you call him, tell me what this means."

"It means they're trying to scare you, play with you. Get you to focus on the wrong thing while they carry out their plan. Don't let them win, but, Halley, I have to get this to somebody right away."

She nodded. Morgan called J.J., who promised to

send one of the guard detail.

"Hey, Morgan, you hear from Stanley yet today?" J.J. asked him.

"Nope. Not a word. I take it you haven't, either."

"That's right. And Taylor hasn't talked to him in two days."

"Probably means he's in real deep."

"Should I try to call him?"

"He's smart enough to turn off his phone when he has to, but let's not take that risk. Have your guys looking out for him, both here and outside the entrance. And text me when you find him, okay?"

"Sure. Sending someone down now."

The knock at the door confirmed J.J.'s promise. Morgan handed him the note.

The guard read it over and glanced at the roses. "Those better come out of here."

Morgan hadn't thought about that.

The guard turned to the makeup artist. "Ma'am, were these in here when you got here?"

"Yes, they were."

"I'm sorry, but we're switching rooms. There's a smaller green room down at the end of the hallway. You take that. Don't know how it happened, but we gotta sweep the entire backstage now."

Morgan spoke into a microphone on his lapel. Then he turned to Halley. "I'm going to punch someone's lights out for this," he said.

Two other guards arrived to escort the three of them down the hall. Morgan told J.J. what had happened. The flowers were whisked away and a large German Shepherd was lead in by a leash.

"This room been searched?" Morgan asked.

Both guards nodded. Halley sat down and resumed her makeup. Morgan excused himself to the outer hallway, the guards right behind him, and watched them blend into the considerable traffic of technicians go back and forth. A young girl with headphones on arrived. "I'm Dorey, production assistant. She's on in thirty minutes. Either of you need anything?"

"Yes, I'd like to know how those roses got in her dressing room?"

"She had a pass."

"Who did?"

"The lady with the flowers. She had a backstage pass."

Morgan turned to open the door and found it locked. He kicked it in. Halley was on the ground. The makeup artist bent over her, ready to inject her with a needle. Morgan gripped her wrist, twisted the woman's arm backward, and heard a satisfying cracking sound as he fractured the two bones in her forearm. She screamed, and immediately Morgan twisted her neck and dropped her lifeless body to the ground.

Halley had walked backward like a crab, her eyes wide and filled with horror. Her fingers rubbed her neck, pulling off a silk scarf that had been used in an attempt to strangle her. Morgan picked her up in his arms. A small crowd had gathered outside the door he'd smashed in.

Halley was still in shock. "Are you okay?" he asked her. "Did she hurt you?"

"No, but how—I don't understand."

Morgan recognized the signs of emotional trauma common after a physical attack. "Get her some water right now. And can you quickly get another artist?"

"No! No more of that," Halley protested. I don't want anyone here I don't know."

"That's smart thinking. Maybe you could use—" He opened up the artist's bag and found a small bomb made very crudely. One thing he did recognize was the plastic bag of ammonium nitrate strapped with duct tape to what looked like an incendiary device. He threw his jacket over the whole kit, and handed it to one of the guards outside. "Dispose of this as quickly as possible and then get back here." The guard began a near jog, weaving his way around the stage crews until he exited a manned door. Less than a minute later, they all heard an explosion.

"Oh my God. I hope he's okay," cried Halley.

"We're going back to Plan A," said Morgan. He

carried Halley back to the original dressing room. The dogs were being lead out.

"We're clear, Morgan," one of the security detail whispered.

Dorey handed her a cold bottled water and then said, "Let me get my purse. I have some stage makeup in it."

"Dorey, forget it," Halley blurted out, grabbing her arm. "Would you make sure the teleprompter is working correctly? Tell me what they've cued up first."

"You got it. I'll be back in two minutes."

Morgan took her in his arms. "Baby, we don't have to do this. Should we call this off?"

"No. I'm not going to let them do this to us! I'm not quitting!"

Morgan's phone rang with J.J.'s number.

"Okay, San Jose P.D. is on the makeup woman, and the bomb squad investigators are on what's left of the kit. No one hurt." J.J. briefed him.

"That's good news."

"Fast work there, stud. Anyway, we have another problem. We've found Stanley, barely alive. His throat was cut. They're taking him to the hospital, but we're not sure he's going to make it."

"Oh shit." Morgan noted Halley was hearing part of the conversation.

"Good thing we had paramedics on scene already. I

think he'd not have a chance otherwise. I've got to send one of the guard detail to stay with him."

"Does Taylor know?"

"Yes. He's still in Stockton. Said Stanley agreed to drive someone to the event."

"Any idea who?"

"He said it was a couple. So there are two more we haven't got to yet. He's found someone who is willing to cooperate and is getting more information as we speak."

"So nobody saw this happening?"

"Stanley was just standing in line to get in, and evidently they got him from behind. Witnesses just thought he'd tripped. So now we're one guard and one man short. That changes things."

"And we are looking for a female as well as a man," Morgan whispered, watching Halley become calm, morphing into a woman of steel right before his eyes.

"Yup, and ninety-five percent of the audience is women. She's gonna blend in, for sure."

Morgan was amazed Halley wasn't more fearful now than before. But if anything, her resolve had grown. Her jaw locked tight. Her eyes didn't waver, nor filled with emotion. She was set. All set. Locked and loaded.

J.J. asked again, "You sure she wants to go on and do this? I think it's folly, myself. That's two close calls already in one night."

Morgan held the phone up to Halley's mouth. "Your call, sweetheart. Tell him what you want."

Halley blurted out, "It's showtime, J.J. Now don't ask me again."

CHAPTER 22

HALLEY BRUSHED OFF her skirt as best she could. She'd ask the cameraman not to film that side. She combed her hair quickly, reapplied lipstick, and tried to take some of the sweat off her face from the altercation. Morgan watched her in the mirror, from behind.

"Wicked beautiful. I can't believe you're doing this."

"What am I going to do, run? Would you run?"

Touche.

"Besides, I got the best of the best at my side. We've found a bomb, disabled an assassin, discovered we're still looking for two more people, and found some holes in the operation that I'm sure you've plugged up. There's nothing I can do except give the crowd what they want to hear, and the bad guys a heart attack."

He grabbed her, pulling her face toward him with both hands. "Remember, I'm here. I'm not going anywhere."

He wound up with half her red lipstick all over his handsome kisser. She wasn't going to tell him, just let him wear the red until someone else blabbed. He'd like that, she thought.

"You have the computer?"

"Yup, right here." He pointed to the chair. "Won't leave my side."

Dorey popped her head in, handing her the headset she'd use on stage and adjusting the battery pack under her jacket on her skirt waistband. "Can you test for me, Halley?"

"Can you hear me okay?"

Dorey nodded when she got confirmation the engineer had her signal. "Okay, it's time."

"They got the teleprompter set up with the notes?"

"Oh, sorry! Yes. They're all set."

Dorey opened the door and searched right and left. She took Halley's arm, leading her in the opposite direction from the bevy of police at the end of the hall and up a half-flight of stairs to the stage wings. Halley had a vice grip on Morgan's hand, but he stayed right with her. She took strength from the way he gripped her hand back, almost to the point of it hurting.

Gibril was there and greeted her with a big smile. "What the hell's going on?"

"I'll tell you later. Thanks for coming. How's your

niece?"

"I can't find her. But there are just too many people. It was a madhouse getting back here."

"Good." Morgan leaned in. He waved at Gibril, who looked totally confused.

"Jeff? Or was it Hank?"

"Very good, neither. I'm Morgan. Halley's ex." He extended his hand. "Nice to formally meet you Gibril."

Halley tried to concentrate on the first lines of her speech, but saw it was Gibril who told Morgan about the lipstick, even handing him one of his monogramed handkerchiefs.

The cameraman sidled up to her. "Announcing you now. Get ready."

"Don't film this side." She turned and showed him the dark smudge from her fall in the dressing room.

"Not a problem, Halley."

They heard the announcer and then the applause. Spotlights were turned on. She sucked in air and remembered her vow to make it the best speech of her life. Like doing a spacewalk, she let go of Morgan's hand, her last tether to safety, and floated out into the light, walking on the rose petals she'd had laid out under her feet. The heady aroma calmed her. She waved to the crowd as a sea of cell phone flashes went off. She took the time to wave into the upper decks at the very corners, and scanned the front row, shaking a few hands of people she recognized from her previous events.

"Say it with me right now and make it count." She hesitated so everyone could get ready, and in unison, the whole building roared, "Ladies, start your engines."

The cheering was raucous and it did help ease her jitters, which had started the second she'd let go of Morgan's hand.

"Do I have a tale to tell you tonight!"

Again she received applause. She heard Morgan's phone ring and she turned to see him put it to his ear.

"I don't know if you heard that, but would you please turn off your cell phones?"

She was going to wink at Morgan, but he was engrossed in his call. So she took another deep breath.

"Tonight, you and I are going to stand for the impossible. We are going to do something completely ridiculous. We're going to change our lives forever. *All* our lives," she said as she pointed with a sweeping arm to the crowd.

Again, the applause and even whistles filled the room.

"Show me by hands, who knows how to do that—whistle?"

Several arms shot up.

"I've always wanted to learn how to whistle like a man. You've got to teach me, okay? That's the other seminar we do. Whistling in the face of danger. Laughing at our fears and becoming the best we that we can be. Who's for that?"

Hands waved, and again, the audience loved it.

"Would you believe there are those who are afraid of new ideas? Who don't think women should have the kind of power they've really had for centuries. Who do you think gave birth to all the great thinkers, inventors, and doers in the world, huh?"

The audience shouted out, "*women.*"

"We all know the Ginger Rogers of the female population, don't we? The ones who keep up with Fred Astaire, except they do it backwards and in high heels, right? Well, tonight we all are going to be Ginger Rogers. We're going to dance our way into the history books."

She waited for the clapping to stop.

"Tonight, we're going to do something that others said couldn't be done."

She looked above her, saw faces of men dressed in uniforms, and the basket of rose petals that would fall at the end of her talk. She looked to the right and to the left of the stage, making eye contact with the cameramen, Morgan, Gibril, and Dorey.

"Are you ready?"

The audience shouted "*ready!*"

"Now, if I don't look entirely perfect tonight, we've

had a little altercation backstage. All ably taken care of, thank you." She bowed to Morgan and smiled at Gibril, who looked shocked again.

"There are those who want to silence me, not because I'm telling you anything that's bad for you or for our planet, but because I bring you a message of hope, understanding for what you've been through, and a promise to stay by your side as long as I can be."

Halley decided it was time to pay attention to the teleprompter, which was still stuck on, *'Welcome to Success Summit, ladies.'*

"And you know who taught me that? You taught me that. With your outpouring of love, your willingness to become something greater than the already-great you that exists. Because of our collective stubbornness to continually learn, transform, and spread the joy and hope that is all around us."

The teleprompter wasn't moving. Was she going to have to wing the whole forty-five minutes? She was about to launch into her Definition of Success.

At last, the words on the two sides moved, and in her greeting's place, someone had hand-written a message, that read,

You lead women on a path to their own destruction.

CHAPTER 23

"—And he said she'd been promised in marriage to the cleric, but refused. He had her kidnapped and raped her."

Morgan had one eye on Halley under the glowing lights of the stage, and the other on Gibril, who was clearly mesmerized with her presence. He'd found he couldn't hate the man anymore.

Taylor continued. "Well, she got pregnant, and—get this—this guy told me she had an abortion. She'd wanted to go to college, have a life like so many of her friends had in California. A career. Her family found out about it, and—"

Morgan could see where all this was going, and it connected to Gibril. Taylor was jabbering about Gibril's niece. Morgan whispered to the cameraman, who was not happy.

"You are panning the audience, right? Anyone show up with their head covered?"

The cameraman spoke into his microphone to the other camera, and Morgan heard the term asshole come up.

Just then, Halley turned to the side and pointed at the teleprompter. With Taylor squawking in one ear, he and Gibril read the note on the screen and gasped in unison.

"Taylor, get off the fucking phone and tell J.J. something's wrong. Halley just got a threat on the teleprompter." He hung up and was about to grab Halley and drag her off the stage when the cameraman pulled his arm.

The woman in the front row dressed in a light aqua headscarf draped around her shoulders. Underneath, she wore a raincoat with pockets, open down the front. As she began to rise, she opened her coat wide, revealing she was packed with explosives.

"Fatima!" Gibril shouted and headed toward Halley.

Morgan was trying to get her to run back toward him, but she was transfixed. Almost in slow motion, she looked between Gibril and the pretty girl in the front row.

"J.J. We need a shooter quick. Front row. Headscarf." Morgan commanded.

Before he could finish, a crack rang out, and Fatima fell to the ground with a mortal head wound. Her hand gripped a trigger device.

The bomb squad couldn't wait for an evacuation, and panic set in all around the stage. One very brave agent searched her setup and wiring, peeled the device from her now limp hand, and unscrewed the cylinder, letting a couple of batteries fall to the ground. He snipped two wires, on her chest, nodded to his backup behind a shield, and the two of them moved Fatima out of the arena.

It was over in less than thirty seconds. Halley was still in the light, but her audience was in bold retreat.

"Please, ladies, calm down. Slow down and be safe."

But the thunderous stampede would not be abated. Several guards were culling through the audience, helping people who were tripping over the thick carpeting and trying to climb over the padded seats to get to the exit. All the doors had been opened to allow everyone to get out.

Morgan heard J.J. report that the control room had been secured. They'd arrested the young disciple of the Imam.

He also got a report that no one who wasn't supposed to be there was on the catwalk above. All the doors backstage were reported secured.

The event was over. Halley slumped to the canvas floor, pulling off her headset. The cameraman came up behind her and kept filming. Morgan yanked his arm and barked, putting his face right in the lens.

"Turn that fucking thing off." would be the last anyone would see of the night's event.

He came over to Halley and knelt beside her, pulling her to his chest. Only then did she start to cry.

"I didn't get to finish," she sniffled.

"No, but you got the job done." He squeezed her hard, placed his hands beneath her jaw and tilted her to look at him. "Message delivered, Halley. You were right. Nothing will ever be the same again. You showed up. You did your part, and the fucking message was delivered."

He kissed her tear-stained lips gently until she began to unthaw and rise to him. The woman with the hair trigger had the strongest will to live and also the strongest libido he'd ever known.

"I'm here, Halley. I'm always going to be here, right beside you."

Gibril walked slowly over to the two of them, covered in blood. He too was crying.

"I am so sorry," he said as he bowed his head, touching both their heads.

Halley grabbed his hand and used it to lever herself up. She placed her palms on his cheeks and wiped his tears away with her thumbs like Morgan had done to her so many times. "You didn't know, Gibril. They used you. I am so sorry. I am sorry for your family.

Please give my prayers to her mother."

IN A LITTLE beauty parlor in Stockton, Imam Al-Moustafi soaked in a tub with rose bath salts. His dead eyes watched the events on the news from a flat screen mounted at the foot of the tub. The drama played out there wasn't anything he'd expected.

The water dripped peacefully from a rusty, leaky faucet, and the room filled with steam. It wouldn't be long now before they came for him. His guards outside had been sent away earlier so he could savor his victory in private. His weakened condition left him lethargic as he watched his betrothed, the child already ripped from her body, receive the communion of the sharp-shooter and fall to the ground.

In the end, she'd done it to save her family from disgrace, with the protection he'd offered them. Otherwise, he suggested he could take her little sister. She knew she'd never get away from the community and it was her duty to fix the stain she'd caused.

It wasn't going to be up to him to spin it like it was a successful mission, though. Perhaps if he were healthier, he thought. But life had ceased to be for him when he found out that she'd defiled herself and him by killing his child.

Could he escape? Perhaps. Did he want to? He wasn't sure.

The door burst open, and the redhead demon boy entered, his eyes just as red. With two powerful gloved hands he grabbed his neck, forcing him under water. He chose not to struggle or fight. He would have rather died fighting, but the statement was made. Now the infidels knew that there was no problem finding people to carry out the plan. If he was gone, another would take his place. And then another and another. It was going to be a war of wills. Whoever stopped fighting first would lose.

The water was milky from his skin cells and the bath salts so that the bubbles his lips released looked like those he'd blown as a child when the young serviceman had given him the purple plastic bottle with the wand. This man was a soldier too. Not the same one, but this man would bring him peace. He had opened the Golden Gates for him. His soul would be going to Allah, and indeed, everything was good and as it should be.

CHAPTER 24

IN THE AFTERMATH of the event, news crews didn't take long to arrive. The film taken by the freelance cameraman had gone viral on social media, even in all its graphic display, just minutes after the shooting.

Morgan managed to get her out of the auditorium, whisking her away to a suite provided by the Grand Fordham itself. It was on the opposite side of the property, facing the bay, with no view of the auditorium.

They told her she could stay as long as she liked. All she wanted was a shower and a good night's sleep with Morgan at her side, if he could be. So many questions and interviews he'd have to do, but in the end, they'd acquiesced and let them leave with the promise to be available in the morning. They also were told Stanley was going to pull through, due to the quick actions of the paramedics at the scene.

"Where would you like me to take you next?" he

asked her as he dried off. She was halfway disappointed he hadn't made love to her in the shower. But his tenderness and attentiveness, she appreciated. It made her smile to think he'd been acting like Gibril. He was a gentleman, careful to treat her like the delicate flower she was not. But for however long it would last, she liked it. Here was another side of the man she knew she'd always loved. Even before she'd met him.

She slung her towel over the bar on the shower door and walked naked to the bed, thinking.

"You know? Gibril had this client once, just for a short time. He said the guy had met the girl of his dreams and had bought an island in the Caribbean and was going to just drop out. Somewhere near Antigua.

"I've been there. Admiral Nelsons' old dockyard is at English Bay. Beautiful place."

"He even showed me some of the pictures of that bay, the blue water and that street sign planted in the sand with directions to places like Berlin, New York, and Rio. He told me you could have a cheeseburger and a beer in Paradise."

"What happened to the client? Did Gibril ever go there and meet him?"

"No. He said he just disappeared one day."

"Maybe he was successful. Maybe he took the girl and he lived on that island Happily Ever After."

"I'd like to think so, except that he left a lot of

money in his account. Gibril's been waiting nearly two years for him to return."

"That's a fun story."

"Morgan, would you take me to Paradise?"

He slipped under the covers to join her. His long hard body pulsed with heat and desire. Hers caught hold of the rhythm and her heart started racing in anticipation.

"Close your eyes, Halley. I'm going to take you to Paradise tonight and every day for the rest of your life. Will you promise to never bring me back if we get lost?"

She wrapped her arms about his neck. "That I can do."

She accepted his deep kiss and then how his hungry mouth traveled down her neck, then back up to her ear as he positioned his groin, begging for entry.

He whispered, "I'm nearly there right now."

If you enjoyed this book, won't you consider leaving a review? Thanks so much and may all your dreams be happily ever after.

But wait! There's more! Did you know the creators of Sleeper SEALs have come up with a new series?

That's right, Silver SEALs! Starting February 5, 2019 the first book in the Silver SEALs, SEAL Love's Legacy, will launch. Buy it here.

sharonhamiltonauthor.com/seal-loves-legacy

Here's an excerpt from SEAL Love's Legacy:

CHAPTER 1

G ARRETT TIERNEY, U.S. Navy SEAL Commander (Ret.), was having a good day mucking out his chicken coops on an especially warm, autumn afternoon in Northern California. Even his eight-year-old rooster—the meanest animal he'd ever met—had left him alone. Maude, sold to him as a pullet with the two-dozen other Americanas for his new free-range egg venture, would normally be attempting to stab him in the calves after taking a flying leap several feet into the air. Garrett vowed one day he'd put a shovel to his neck. It wasn't his fault the bird was misnamed, but he figured Maude saw it otherwise.

He wore his knee-high muck boots just in case.

His handyman, Geronimo, hauled the manure-filled wheelbarrow to the acre vegetable patch Garrett lovingly tended. They were going to plant some new curly-leaf Kale and red cabbage starts in the mixture later, before sunset.

Tierney rested a bit on his shovel, feeling the strain in his lower back from an old injury occurring on one of those midnight HALO jumps in Afghanistan years ago. At forty-four and holding, his body was still as strong as some of the young froglets, or new Team Guys, he occasionally saw. Except for his back. But he could live with that. In fact, he was damn proud of it.

He surveyed his ten acres, all flat and useable, with the small winter creek going through the lower boundary that would fill up soon and need some repair work. It was a nice little slice of Heaven, tamed and carved out of the old apple orchard long since gone. He'd used some of the old wood to make rustic cabinets and countertops inside the bungalow he and some friends had built.

Geronimo returned with the red wheelbarrow.

Tierney always spoke English to the man. "I think maybe we got two more to go. Then I can start spreading shavings."

"Your garden looks good, Commander. You plant just in time. We got rain coming tomorrow," he said, pointing at the bright blue sky being invaded by large, grey puffy clouds.

"Perfect!"

He was spreading pine shavings and adjusting the chicken boxes inside the night coop when he heard the phone ring inside the house. No one ever called him on that line, except for telemarketers, so he let the answering machine pick up.

The hens began jockeying for position, scratching

the floor and testing their butts in the new shavings. Maude chased several of them and scored with three, one right after the other. He laughed at the rooster, who stopped and angled his head, as if listening to him.

"You know what they say, Maude, a little more foreplay and less rape? It would make for a nicer hookup. You don't have to sweet talk them, but the jumping on their backs, biting their necks, and running their faces into the mud, that's not cool."

But what the hell do I know? He'd had his share of girlfriends, but nothing stuck.

Maude looked in the opposite direction and crowed, flapping his wings and getting as tall as his twenty inches could get him. If he behaved himself, he might die a natural death, as Tierney let most his senior hens do. He kept a side yard for the older girls where Maude couldn't get them.

Tierney enjoyed chatting about chicken sex with Maude, because it was a one-way conversation, which is what any conversation on sex should be, he thought.

He'd done it all in his twenty-five years in the Navy. Went in as a dumb kid right out of high school, made it through BUD/S, did five back-to-back tours on two Teams. When he almost got in trouble, he was recommended and went to OCS and still actively deployed. He'd never wanted to be anything but a Master Chief, but the Navy had other plans. Because of his extensive combat experience, Tierney was one of the most respected amongst his peers as he rose to the rank of Lieutenant Commander.

But now I'm still a dumb kid. An older dumb kid.

Geronimo had asked him recently why he never got married.

"You *do* know it isn't the man's choice, right? I never got married because no woman ever chose me."

They'd had a good laugh at that.

Life was pretty perfect. If it wasn't for his back. He bet he could still bark orders and make men pee themselves, run faster than the tadpoles, and qualify expert if he tried, though. The way Tierney figured, he'd seen enough of the world in his first twenty-five years of adulthood. Now it was time to quit running things and start just living with the rest of it.

Of course, there was always something to fix— some issue with the well, the septic system, fencing, or his solar panels. Something needed paint, something broken on one of his tractors or splitters or his beat-up farm truck, an issue with the plumbing, or a light that wouldn't work. That kept him pretty busy.

At night, he'd read or crash on his huge leather couch that fit him like a second skin, watching old war movies because it helped him sleep. He had his half-Doberman, half-Pit Bull rescue dog, Snooker, and a litter of cats in the barn he could never catch, who kept the mouse and rat population at bay.

He needed a woman like he needed a second dick. She'd just get in the way.

But on some of those cold, dark evenings, he missed the Brotherhood, if he was totally honest with himself. He could do without the bleeding and dying. But accomplishing the missions and saving some innocent lives, or one of his own guys? That shit was fun. Making it out alive just in time and blowing stuff up, he could do that until he was eighty, maybe longer. His sister had called him an old Boy Scout. Well, that's how a woman thought.

And that's why he was still single.

GARRET HAD JUST stepped out of the shower when he heard his phone ring. Wrapping himself in a bathsheet, he padded barefoot to the kitchen, checking the windows for any evidence of outside visitors. He thought Geronimo was long gone, but sometimes, his helper would work late sharpening the gardening tools in preparation for the next day's chores.

He waited, never answering without knowing who was on the other line first. Those who knew him understood this. Those who didn't, well, they shouldn't be calling his home phone.

"Come on, Tierney, you asshole. Pick up."

He recognized the voice immediately.

"Commander, what can I do you for?" Holding his breath, he knew it wasn't a social call. Former SEAL Commander Silas Branson was not one to chit-chat. And he knew the world had to be at an end before he ever would get a call from him.

"I'm with DHS now, and I got something you might be interested in."

Tierney didn't say a word, exhaling with control so Branson wouldn't detect he was working on his nerves. He inhaled again, holding his breath until dark circles started appearing in his eyes.

"Tierney? You there?"

"I'm all here, Commander. What I didn't leave over in the sandbox."

"You came out better than most."

"And that's a fact. Now what could possibly interest me more than getting drunk on a beautiful California sunset, working in my garden, gathering blue and green eggs, planting my three dozen veggies in the morning, and then maybe getting laid before sunset?"

"That's a tall order. But there was a time when your country came before all that."

He didn't know what to say, because anything that might pop out would be disrespectful of the good old U.S. of A., to Commander Branson, or to himself. So, he waited. But it pissed him off no end. It was one of those wounds that woundn't heal, like he didn't deserve his time off after what he'd seen in the theater of war.

"I'll take that as a yes," Branson mumbled.

"Yes, what?"

"Yes, you're interested."

"And how the hell did you get that?

"Because you would have hung up on me, that's how."

AFTER THE PHONE call, he shuffled back to the bathroom with the wet bath sheet still draped across his hips like he was some Roman Legionnaire at a bath in Carthage. He examined himself in the partially fogged mirror. He knew he looked old. His lines were the same, but deepened, especially the ones around his eyes and mouth. He had some grey hair making a showing at his temples some woman had recently said looked sexy. He didn't think so but was against altering the natural color of his hair.

If God made it, I'm gonna wear it.

His hands didn't shake anymore, like they did the last year he served on the Teams. He knew that was from getting more sleep than he'd ever gotten before in his life and from all the outdoor work he did. Building the house had been good for him. Tilling the soil had brought him back to life. Rescuing Snooker from the shelter was the cherry on top. He had his land, his dwelling, and, with Snooker, he had his family. He was taken care of and could just live this way until he was ready to check out.

He was *not* ready for another mission. He didn't have to prove to himself or anyone else he had what it took, that he could still outrun those little froglets and eat and drink them under the table.

So then why in God's green earth had he said yes?

THE TICKET HAD arrived online like Branson said it would. Two days later, he disembarked from the flight to D.C., meeting in a "need to know" location somewhere in the bowels of the city. Stepping out into the terminal, it smelled the same. The mix of races and body sweat overpowered him. The pace was faster than he was used to. Everyone was so busy, each with their own agendas. Some were harmless. Most of them in D.C. were dangerous, at least for those who had to go do the work the Head Sheds of government manufactured.

Commander Branson was a cool dude with warm brown eyes. He was disarming the way those eyes could look so sad. He'd lost his son not more than three years back. Garrett knew what it was like to lose family. But losing a child might be something a man couldn't ever get over. Every time he looked at Branson, he saw the pain the man tried so hard to cover up.

But what really stood out was that Branson had bulked up. At 6'3", he'd always been one of the big guys, but now he looked like a fuckin' transformer. His small waist and broad shoulders were tight, without an ounce of extra fat anywhere. Cut and lean, Garrett guessed the man still weighed 220.

He leaned against a shiny black Ford F-150 Raptor, and the Military Model to boot. No mistaking the fact that Silas wasn't into hauling soil or chicken feed or pulling a trailer or tiller out in a field somewhere.

"Son of a bitch, Commander, you haven't aged a year since we last saw each other. You on steroids?"

"Nah, don't touch those things. Besides, you were drunk, Tierney, and you had that little muffin top on your arm, the one with the—" He demonstrated the size of the bridesmaid's upper torso.

"Shut up." Garrett never was apologetic he loved girls with curves, the more the better, as long as they could be athletic in bed. He didn't see it as a flaw in a woman and didn't understand how some men did. "So how you doin'?" he added as they shook, their eyes connecting.

"Jeez, Tierney, your mitts are like sandpaper. Must work well for those handjobs."

His gesture was thankfully obscure.

"I'm a farmer now. Raising chickens, planting a garden, going to bed early. If the apocalypse comes, I'm set. Even learned how to make bread. As long as I can defend it, I can stay there forever even if the world goes to hell."

"Until some asshole decides to blow up California."

They shared a hearty chuckle.

An airport traffic police whistled for them to move on, which they both heard and very publicaly ignored. There was still that chip on their shoulders from bar fights and disputes with other dispensers of authority.

A brisk fall wind blew through Garrett's bones. D.C. could be warm this time of year, but today, it was definitely not. Or maybe he was nervous.

"Get in," Branson barked as he rounded to the driver side.

Garrett dropped his duffel into the rear seat and climbed inside a second before Branson gunned the beast and did a two-lane change without signaling.

"I can see you're still working on your reputation, Commander." Branson had crashed his pickup during BUD/S and was nearly rolled back. He'd been stuck with the nickname Crash ever since.

"Haven't had even a ticket since, I'll have you know. Not that I haven't been close."

Garrett stared straight ahead and allowed the breech of traffic and noise to sink in. He'd forgotten how uncomfortable he was in crowds with too many moving parts. He knew the signs. It was early PTSD.

He stared at his hands and they were as steady as granite.

"So where are we headed?"

"Just sit back and relax, Tierney. What we have to say has to be done in controlled space."

Holy hell. What was I thinking?

"So you're DHS now?" he asked.

"Don't you have ears?"

"What? You thinking I'm wearing a wire? With all this activity around us, how could anyone—?"

"Just humor me. We'll be there in a few."

Garrett started to get pissed now. He didn't like this part of government work, the having to be careful about who was listening and what it meant. The not knowing what was behind that smile, the turn of the cheek, or the way someone moved their hands. A stance would trigger him in those days. Now it all came flooding back. He'd underestimated his readiness for this. He should just level with Branson and get back to California.

"You know, Silas, I'm not at all sure I did the right thing coming out here. I've been off the grid for so long, out of the game. I've turned into my mother's hippie dreams. This place doesn't do anything for me except make me want to stop at the bathroom."

Branson gave him a grin and readjusted his military-issue sunglasses. Without looking back at him, he said, "And that's why you're perfect for this job, Garrett. You were the first one I thought of."

So much for secrets.

"In about five minutes, you're gonna have a nice, clean men's room to use, my brother."

It had been a half-hearted try, Garrett realized too late. Now he was sounding like a whiny kid. No one forced him to take that ticket and get on the plane. To wash all his clothes, clean his weapons and go to the target range yesterday and not today so he wouldn't have any residue that security checks would pick up and question him about. He'd checked out all his bills and made sure Snooker had enough food so Geronimo could feed and tend to him while he was away. Those were the things he used to do before deployments. It set off in motion the rest of the things he would need for a mission.

His mind had to be like steel, focused and hard. He had to prune and clip his emotions like he did his beard this morning, being careful not to draw blood when he shaved. He had eyes in the back of his head as he left his driveway, making sure he hadn't attracted someone's special attention. He turned off the auto-answer feature on his home phone, so it would just ring, like he was out in the garden and couldn't come in to answer. Nothing was to look like he would be gone for any length of time. He didn't need to have anyone know he wasn't there to retrieve a message or pay a bill.

In the old days, he didn't hesitate. One step led to the next and the next until he was in full battle gear, sound and ready to react when the time came. Just like he'd been trained. He'd deployed without even knowing what country they'd step out onto when they arrived, so why was this spooking him so much?

He was still the same man. He was ready. He could handle it. He'd seen enough death and dying, blood covering himself and others around him to be ready. He'd held the dying, the men he wanted to save. He'd made love to women trying to excise his demons and only heard the screams of war instead. Intense lovemaking was a close second, but it didn't dull his memories or the understanding of how fragile life was. He'd tasted the sweet efforts of his home-grown cooking and understood now why he fought so hard. But he fought before he even knew any of that. So why was now so different?

It wasn't.

"You miss those days, Garrett?" Branson asked him as the truck droned on.

"What days? The weddings? The funerals? The—?"

A memory flashed by him. He was holding Connor Lambert in his arms, and although Connor was a big man, it was harder to control his crying than to hold the man's dying body. They shared that look that they'd see each other again, and if it was reversed, Connor would have held him until his last breath was taken. They didn't have to speak; they just looked. It was afterward when the tears and the regrets of not telling him what it was going to feel like missing his best friend began. Nothing came close to that day. Not the day his father was killed in service when Garrett was a boy, not the day his mother gave up her struggle with cancer in the midst of her grief, and not the day his sister went off with some guy she met and never returned. Connor was the only family he'd had. That day would forever be embedded in his psyche.

Damn, Branson!

"I try not to, Si." He wondered if he was too blunt. "I don't miss what we did. We never knew why, so that doesn't figure. I miss the guys, especially the ones who didn't come home."

Branson was quiet, chewing on something, locking his jaws, and then biting his lip. "I hear you. The Boneyard of Bone Frogs. That's a scary place."

He was getting irritated again. "I really didn't come out all this way to talk about that. Most days, I just take what comes."

"Yeah, I know."

They remained silent the rest of the way to the three-story glass office building. The sign out front read *Office of Health, Education and Welfare.* Garrett turned to his buddy. Before he could say anything, Silas interrupted his thoughts.

"Hang in there. I gotta get you passed at the gate. Just be yourself."

Garrett gave him a goofy, cross-eyed grin and drooled.

"Nice."

They drove into a line of cars waiting to clear a sentry station. Garrett thought it was unusual this building would be guarded by a Marine contingent. He signed for the pass that was issued, and he clipped it to the front of his shirt while the young sentry watched carefully. They were shown where to park—in the precise number they were given.

"All will be explained, Tierney. Very soon now."

Garrett noticed the uniforms first. He counted three branches of service represented, including a Navy Vice Admiral, who addressed Branson and frowned at Tierney. He was not given an introduction.

They peeled off into a large room manned by a secretary who logged them in, made note of the information on Garrett's visitor's badge, and then asked him for any electronic devices he was carrying. He handed her his cell with the cracked screen. She asked them if they wanted water or coffee, and he accepted a cold bottle of water. Then she buzzed them in.

He'd been in controlled rooms before. This one was not as nice as some of the ones he'd been in at the State Department. The long table down the middle was made up of various colors of government-issue grey and tan smaller tables, lined end to end. The chairs were also a mismatch. He saw the computer screen lights peeking behind cabinet doors and knew this could be a war room if the occasion warranted it. A wiped-clean whiteboard was off to the side with two markers in the tray below.

"Sit," Branson commanded.

Garrett did so, unscrewing the top of his water and downing half of it. Branson took a delicate sip from his bottle.

"You need a restroom, first? Sorry. Should have asked you earlier."

"Is this going to take long?" Garrett asked.

"Depends on you, but I don't think so."

"Let's get the party started, then."

"I'm going to just give you a little background. I've been with DHS for about two years now. They recruited me just after—"

"I'm sorry about your boy, Commander."

"No more 'Commander.' Please call me Silas, or Branson. We don't identify as former military unless we're known. Understood?"

"Sure."

"My wife left me, which was the last straw. I wanted to go back to the teams in the worst way, but you know how the Navy is. They got eyes even in the men's room, I think. I'd have to re-qualify, and I had a back injury I'd been covering up. But this injury kept me out." He pointed to his heart.

Garrett felt his blood pressure rise. Branson'd had a string of bad luck. He wondered how he would be able to deal with that double tragedy. It was one of the reasons he wasn't drawn toward the altar himself.

"Look, Branson, I just want to say, I've got huge respect for you and how you've dealt with all this."

"Shut up, Tierney. I didn't bring you all the way out here to get sympathy from you—especially you of all people."

Garrett considered whether he should continue and decided he did, for his own piece of mind. "I just want to say that I'm glad you've found something—"

"Something to believe in again?" The smile on Branson's face seemed brittle.

"Not exactly. But go ahead. I'll shut up." Garrett crossed his arms and leaned back in his chair, determined to keep his mouth shut and keep his emotions clipped.

"We've had some disasters recently, mostly because they hired the wrong men and women for the job. You know how I feel about our brothers on the Teams. That's how I got tasked. They've formed a new division of Homeland Security. We call it Bone Frog Command."

"So everyone dies." Garrett knew that the symbol of the Bone Frog was one of the most sacred symbols of the Teams, equal to the Trident.

"We're pulling guys out of mothballs. Guys who were distinguished SEALs, all Commanders or Lieutenant Commanders. We want men of this caliber to run an inter-departmental team to handle security threats to the homeland. Special projects."

"Mission Impossible? Like the *'Director will disavow any knowledge of you should you fail—'*"

"Everything is a joke to you now, is it? You don't fool me one bit, Tierney. I know you miss the Teams."

Their eyes connected. Garrett knew Branson understood him right down to his toenails.

"You had a rough go with Connor. I remember pulling you out of bars, as did several of your guys. We were relieved when you walked away. You were a danger to yourself and anyone else around you. You were about to blow a decent retirement. I can say this because I was the same way."

He leaned forward and lowered his voice, clasping his hands in front of him. Garrett let him get adjusted.

"This mission is about something so sensitive it

cannot go outside this room should you turn me down. And if I thought you'd do that, I wouldn't have asked you to fly out here. We've had some colossal fuckups lately. We're not sure who we can trust here in D.C. We have some internal threats to our way of life. There are even guys in the Head Shed that think the Teams are a bunch of overgrown footballers who can't get it up anymore. Jealousy is ripe. The stench of politics is everywhere.

"And then there's the public, for whom we fought and died. Views have changed. Sometimes the ones we've saved are no longer grateful, not that we did it for that. But it sucks."

"I don't watch the news so all of this doesn't make sense, Si."

"You're a filthy liar, too, Tierney." He grinned, which made Garrett do the same. Branson continued. "The bad guys are here at home. They've always been out there, but our overburdened police, FBI, HS and other departments are overloaded with organized crime and drug enforcement caseloads, stretched so thin they might catch up in the next century. And we want guys most people wouldn't expect would lead a team *inside the United States* to do some special things. We want guys who get 'er done. In the face of impossible odds."

"Impossible? We never thought anything was impossible."

"Exactly. That's not part of our vocabularity. That's why we want former SEALs. Used to leading a command of misfits from all over the place, welding them into a strong cohesive unit. We need a strike force that goes in, gets the job done, and then fades away into the surf, as the commercial goes. Are you in?"

"Well, it would help if I knew what this impossible feat is."

"Yes, I knew you'd say that. But no can do. So, Garrett Tierney, are you in? You think really long and hard before you answer me because I'm not asking again. And I know I'm asking before you know what the mission is."

Garrett felt the blood rushing to his fingers, which exploded with heat. The pulsing behind his ears sent hissing frequencies to his brain. His gut was empty and wrapping around itself. His balls shrank but his dick was hard. His thighs tensed and wanted to run ten miles or do a hundred pushups. Drips of sweat traveled down the sides of his torso. His breathing was controlled, deep, and his chest full of the excitement of the possibilities being given him.

"Hell yes, I'm in."

You can order **SEAL Love's Legacy here**
sharonhamiltonauthor.com/seal-loves-legacy

Be sure to enjoy all the other books in the Silver SEALs Series. Here's the preorder links to all the books in this new series, in order of their appearance:

Did you enjoy this story? Read through the other stories in the Sleeper SEALs Series by eleven other fantastic military romance authors:

Make sure to pick up ALL the books in the Sleeper SEAL series. These can be read in any order and each stands alone.

Protecting Dakota by Susan Stoker
Slow Ride by Becky McGraw
Michael's Mercy by Dale Mayer
Saving Zola by Becca Jameson
Bachelor SEAL by Sharon Hamilton
Montana Rescue by Elle James
Thin Ice by Maryann Jordan
Grinch Reaper by Donna Michaels
All In by Lori Ryan
Broken SEAL by Geri Foster
Freedom Code by Elaine Levine
Flat Line by J.M. Madden

You can follow us along on the Facebook page with links to all the other authors in this set, as well as ordering information for this novella.

ABOUT THE AUTHOR

NYT and USA Today best-selling author Sharon Hamilton's award-winning Navy SEAL Brotherhood series have been a fan favorite from the day the first one was released. They've earned her the coveted Amazon author ranking of #1 in Romantic Suspense, Military Romance and Contemporary Romance categories, as well as in Gothic Romance for her Vampires of Tuscany and Guardian Angels. Her characters follow a sometimes rocky road to redemption through passion and true love.

Now that he's out of the Navy, Sharon can share with her readers that her son spent a decade as a Navy SEAL, and he's the inspiration for her books.

Her Golden Vampires of Tuscany are not like any vamps you've read about before, since they don't go to ground and can walk around in the full light of the sun.

Her Guardian Angels struggle with the human charges they are sent to save, often escaping their vanilla world of Heaven for the brief human one. You won't find any of these beings in any Sunday school class.

She lives in Sonoma County, California with her husband and her Doberman, Tucker. A lifelong organic gardener, when she's not writing, she's getting *verra verra* dirty in the mud, or wandering Farmers Markets looking for new Heirloom varieties of vegetables and flowers. She and her husband plan to cure their wanderlust (or make it worse) by traveling in their Diesel Class A Pusher, Romance Rider. Starting with this book, all her writing will be done on the road.

She loves hearing from her fans:
Sharonhamilton2001@gmail.com

Her website is:
sharonhamiltonauthor.com

Find out more about Sharon, her upcoming releases, appearances and news from her newsletter, **AND receive a free book** when you sign up for Sharon's newsletter.

Facebook:
facebook.com/SharonHamiltonAuthor

Twitter:
twitter.com/sharonlhamilton

Pinterest:
pinterest.com/AuthorSharonH

Google Plus:
plus.google.com/u/1/+SharonHamiltonAuthor/posts

BookBub:

bookbub.com/authors/sharon-hamilton

Youtube:

youtube.com/channel/UCDInkxXFpXp_4Vnq08ZxMBQ

Soundcloud:

soundcloud.com/sharon-hamilton-1

Sharon Hamilton's Rockin' Romance Readers:

facebook.com/groups/sealteamromance

Sharon Hamilton's Goodreads Group:

goodreads.com/group/show/199125-sharon-hamilton-readers-group

Visit Sharon's Online Store:

sharon-hamilton-author.myshopify.com

Join Sharon's Review Teams:

eBook Reviews:

sharonhamiltonassistant@gmail.com

Audio Reviews:

sharonhamiltonassistant@gmail.com

Life is one fool thing after another.

Love is two fool things after each other.

REVIEWS

PRAISE FOR THE
GOLDEN VAMPIRES OF TUSCANY SERIES

"Well to say the least I was thoroughly surprise. I have read many Vampire books, from Ann Rice to Kym Grosso and few other Authors, so yes I do like Vampires, not the super scary ones from the old days, but the new ones are far more interesting far more human then one can remember. I found Honeymoon Bite a totally engrossing book, I was not able to put it down, page after page I found delight, love, understanding, well that is until the bad bad Vamp started being really bad. But seeing someone love another person so much that they would do anything to protect them, well that had me going, then well there was more and for a while I thought it was the end of a beautiful love story that spanned not only time but, spanned Italy and California. Won't divulge how it ended, but I did shed a few tears after screaming but Sharon Hamilton did not let me down, she took me on amazing trip that I loved, look forward to reading another Vampire book of hers."

"An excellent paranormal romance that was exciting,

romantic, entertaining and very satisfying to read. It had me anticipating what would happen next many times over, so much so I could not put it down and even finished it up in a day. The vampires in this book were different from your average vampire, but I enjoy different variations and changes to the same old stuff. It made for a more unpredictable read and more adventurous to explore! Vampire lovers, any paranormal readers and even those who love the romance genre will enjoy Honeymoon Bite."

"This is the first non-Seal book of this author's I have read and I loved it. There is a cast-like hierarchy in this vampire community with humans at the very bottom and Golden vampires at the top. Lionel is a dark vampire who are servants of the Goldens. Phoebe is a Golden who has not decided if she will remain human or accept the turning to become a vampire. Either way she and Lionel can never be together since it is forbidden.

I enjoyed this story and I am looking forward to the next installment."

"A hauntingly romantic read. Old love lost and new love found. Family, heart, intrigue and vampires. Grabbed my attention and couldn't put down. Would definitely recommend."

PRAISE FOR THE
SEAL BROTHERHOOD SERIES

"Fans of Navy SEAL romance, I found a new author to feed your addiction. Finely written and loaded delicious with moments, Sharon Hamilton's storytelling satisfies like a thick bar of chocolate." —Marliss Melton, bestselling author of the *Team Twelve* Navy SEALs series

"Sharon Hamilton does an EXCELLENT job of fitting all the characters into a brotherhood of SEALS that may not be real but sure makes you feel that you have entered the circle and security of their world. The stories intertwine with each book before...and each book after and THAT is what makes Sharon Hamilton's SEAL Brotherhood Series so very interesting. You won't want to put down ANY of her books and they will keep you reading into the night when you should be sleeping. Start with this book...and you will not want to stop until you've read the whole series and then...you will be waiting for Sharon to write the next one." (5 Star Review)

"Kyle and Christy explode all over the pages in this first book, *[Accidental SEAL],* in a whole new series of SEALs. If the twist and turns don't get your heart jumping, then maybe the suspense will. This is a must read for those that are looking for love and adventure with a little sloppy love thrown in for good measure." (5 Star Review)

PRAISE FOR THE
BAD BOYS OF SEAL TEAM 3 SERIES

"I love reading this series! Once you start these books, you can hardly put them down. The mix of romance and suspense keeps you turning the pages one right after another! Can't wait until the next book!" (5 Star Review)

"I love all of Sharon's Seal books, but *[SEAL's Code]* may just be her best to date. Danny and Luci's journey is filled with a wonderful insight into the Native American life. It is a love story that will fill you with warmth and contentment. You will enjoy Danny's journey to become a SEAL and his reasons for it. Good job Sharon!" (5 Star Review)

PRAISE FOR THE
BAND OF BACHELORS SERIES

"*[Lucas]* was the first book in the Band of Bachelors series and it was a phenomenal start. I loved how we got to see the other SEALs we all love and we got a look at Lucas and Marcy. They had an instant attraction, and their love was very intense. This book had it all, suspense, steamy romance, humor, everything you want in a riveting, outstanding read. I can't wait to read the next book in this series." (5 Star Review)

PRAISE FOR THE
TRUE BLUE SEALS SERIES

"Keep the tissues box nearby as you read *True Blue SEALs: Zak* by Sharon Hamilton. I imagine more than I wish to that the circumstances surrounding Zak and Amy are all too real for returning military personnel and their families. Ms. Hamilton has put us right in the middle of struggles and successes that these two high school sweethearts endure. I have read several of Sharon Hamilton's military romances but will say this is the most emotionally intense of the ones that I have read. This is a well-written, realistic story with authentic characters that will have you rooting for them and proud of those who serve to keep us safe. This is an author who writes amazing stories that you love and cry with the characters. Fans of Jessica Scott and Marliss Melton will want to add Sharon Hamilton to their list of realistic military romance writers." (5 Star Review)

Made in the USA
Las Vegas, NV
05 November 2020

10584306R00166